KYLER KNIGHTLY AND DAMON COLE

CONTINUITY GIRL

NIK MORTON

ALSO FEATURING
WE FELL BELOW THE EARTH

ISBN: 978-1-943035-28-1

www.beattoapulp.com

ACKNOWLEDGMENTS

Many thanks to David for asking yet again.

Thanks to Garnett Elliott for starting me on this time-jaunt!

Lots of love to Jennifer, my editor, wife and friend; and to Hannah, Harry, Darius, and Suri.

The quotations used in the story "We Fell Below the Earth" are from the poetry collection *Celebrations in the Ossuary* by Kyle J. Knapp, and used with permission.

CONTENTS

What has gone before . . .

In our future, Kyler Knightly and his uncle Damon Cole are field agents for Continuity Inc, a private organization that obtained the contract when the government Time Corps was deregulated. CI is dedicated to protecting human history.

They use the Zygma projector to travel through time and must carry a focus object from the period they're targeting.

Kyler is also a dreamer with passive psychic talents, a precognitive.

The head of the group is an Artificial Intelligence character, Sennacherib, which possesses an organic interface, sharing the body of a two-spot octopus in an aquarium tank! Their offices are in the West End of London, a disused theater.

CONTINUITY GIRL

I

Kyler Knightly was in deep, submerged in a precog sleep. He was in that state where he knew it was a dream but it seemed real, where days and weeks could pass in the blinking of a rapid-movement eye.

Shielded from the sun's harmful rays by the soot-stained Plexiglas dome, this broad section of the London skyline shimmered before his eyes, and transformed slowly, uncannily. The Gherkin, the Shard, the O2 dome, the Third Eye, Saint Paul's Cathedral, Tower Bridge, the Scalpel, the Cheesegrater, One Blackfriars (known as the Pregnancy Bulge), the Independence Tower (commonly known as the Brexit Finger), the New Houses of Parliament and Big Ben, they all dissolved to be replaced by classic Roman architecture, an enormous amphitheater, tall blocks of dwellings fronted with Doric columns, aqueducts and viaducts that spanned the river and white marble temples faced with ornate friezes extolling battle triumphs and appeasing gods.

As the buildings metamorphosed, he perceived that the clarity was unsettling.

Sweating, his heart hammering, he surfaced from the dream.

What alarmed him was the fact that this precog event was not experienced with specific apparatus in the precog suite. His mouth was dry, for usually this kind of unaided dream proved to be true.

Leaving his apartment, he hurried to the renovated theater in London's West End, instinctively checking as he traveled: the city was the same as he'd seen when he signed off from his shift yesterday. That meant nothing. His precog dream was an image from the future. Something or someone in the past must have created a massive time-ripple to cause that kind of radical alteration.

When he got there, the stage and assorted sets were eerily silent. "Damon!" he called. "Sennacherib!" Neither his uncle nor the AI responded. He strode purposefully. Yet foreboding hovered over his shoulder, as he passed through Victorian streets and incongruously adjoining science fiction sets. For some time prior to the privatization of the Zygma Project, this theater had been utilized for a variety of Flix movies, and the sets still remained, virtually intact. Indeed, a few of them proved useful, as they provided appropriate focus objects for the jaunts of field agents into the past.

"Your uncle's in a meeting with Sennacherib and Melody," purred a mellifluous voice behind him.

He pivoted. An auburn-haired woman, her hair draped to shoulders, stood in the doorway. Her blue-gray eyes lanced, playful and tantalizing, piercing his heart. She was tall, lithe, dressed in a tight-fitting purple cat-suit that broadcast her estimable figure's dimensions. He guessed that she was in her twenties.

"I don't know you," he mumbled. "Are you new here?"

"Tertia Beynon," she said, extending her hand. "Continuity girl."

They shook. Her fingers were long; she had a firm grip.

"Continuity …?"

"My role is varied," she said. "When they made Flix, I was responsible for ensuring that everything and everyone was in the correct place from take to take."

"Take?"

"Flix aren't made chronologically, you know. They're filmed in chunks. I have to make sure that one chunk matches in every detail the last or the next one."

"You said 'varied,' I think."

"So I did. I was also responsible for guaranteeing that a time-jaunt did not result in any discrepancy …"

Kyler grinned. "You worked with the Time Corps, then?"

"Until they disbanded and you lot took over."

There wasn't any tone of resentment in her comment. A simple statement of fact. He wondered if she might be useful interpreting his latest precog

3

dream. "Are you aware of any 'discrepancies' you weren't able to rectify?"

She cocked her head to one side. "Why do you ask?"

He countered with, "Why are you here now, since your paymasters have gone?"

"Touché, Mr. …?"

"Knightly. Kyler Knightly."

She flushed. "Knight in shining armor?"

Surprisingly abashed at the allusion, he managed, falteringly, "You—you're not in distress, are you?"

"Actually, I'm not. But history might be …"

II

"Uncle Damon, we have a problem," Kyler said, lifting his gaze from the computer tablet on his lap.

"What's troubling you?"

"I've had a premonition, a dream. The face of London is radically changed."

"Result of a war, do you suppose?"

"No … Strange, but it seemed like Rome had been transplanted."

"Rome? That's mighty odd. No clues?"

"None so far. I've been going through the old records at someone's suggestion."

"Someone?"

"The Time Corps continuity girl …"

His uncle chuckled. "This sounds good. It's about time you had a romantic interest. Girl or woman?"

"Oh, definitely woman," Kyler said, envisioning Tertia's physique.

"And she's obviously from the Flix period?"

"Yes … I'd say Tertia could appear in a movie, too." He jerked himself out of that fanciful reverie. "Anyway, she suggested I look into the Time Corps records, they might give me a clue. Apparently, there were some discrepancies remaining after the takeover."

"You're telling me! Yes, Kyler, that might be a good idea. We already know they left a mess behind, those rogue time-jumpers for example. It's the usual story. The switching of the contract to Continuity Inc. was too fast, by all accounts. That might explain our problems with the AI interfaces, I'd wager. And it might help get to the bottom of your precog dream."

"It isn't a simple matter, Uncle D. There were a number of offshoot departments involved at the time."

"Really? Offshoot how?"

"Language learning academies, archaeological funds, political science colleges, Flix directors, writers and artists …"

"Sounds like you have your work cut out, there." Damon checked his chronometer. "Sorry I can't help you. It seems a bit boring, all that delving, to be honest. I've been slated for a jaunt to 1821, to the island of Saint Helena—lingering worries about the impending death of Napoleon Bonaparte. A French historian has come up with yet another murder theory. I'm to escort him there and back, just to make sure he doesn't alter anything—or save the little emperor's life."

"But what if I need to go on a jaunt while you're away? Who can authorize it?"

"Ahah, you fancy a romantic holiday in Rome, is that it?"

Kyler flushed. "No, be serious. It's business. That precog dream has me worried."

"Confirm it with Sennacherib. You'll get the green light, I'm sure. Take your Tertia with you—and take care."

III

"Any luck, Kyler?" Tertia asked.

He swiveled the viewscreen round for her. "These records have revealed something odd," he observed.

She leaned over him, studying the text. "Oh, I remember Tropes Unlimited."

"What was it?"

"A film and publishing company. They specialized in historical fact and fiction. It was established by four academics who also worked part-time for the Government Time Corps."

"Who were they?"

She jabbed at the screen and another window appeared. "Here they are: Fiction author Mary Ellison, film producer Lucian Matheson, historian Tom Matheson and film director and writer Sebastian Bulmer. I know all of them and worked with them."

Encouraged, he activated a dropdown window and tapped in a series of requests and codes. "Interesting. I've unlocked some hidden files relating to Tropes

Unlimited." He brought up the details and whistled. "Now, that *is* interesting."

Bulmer had compiled a full record of the secret duplication of four Zygma projectors.

"He doesn't show where they put them, though," Tertia said.

"We could probably trace them, if they're still active. The power surge will be a dead giveaway."

She nodded. "I can obtain a surge probe from the props department."

"A real one?" he queried.

"Of course. Props was our term for the quarter-master branch of Time Corps."

"Ah." Kyler nodded. The biography he elicited showed Bulmer's most recent Flix productions were very popular: *The Rise of Rome, Caligula's Concubines,* and the most recent offering, *The Year of the Five Emperors.* "He's quoted as saying he researched his material firsthand."

"How did he square the cost of time-jumps with earning millions of SMUs for himself?"

Kyler shrugged, slowly scrolling down the page. "Blatant misappropriation, frowned on but never punished …"

"I think we're onto something," she said, pointing at fresh text. "Bulmer's next project is scheduled to be *Death on Hadrian's Wall*, prompted by his last film project about the five emperors of 193 AD."

"Five emperors in a year? That's excessive, isn't it? If I recall history correctly, even the Italian governments hadn't changed that frequently."

"It was a time of factions," she said.

"Who were these five?"

She counted off on her fingers. "Pertinax, Didius Julianus, Pescennius Niger, Clodius Albinus and then Septimius Severus."

"All those names mean nothing to me, I'm afraid."

* * *

True to her word, Tertia obtained a surge probe and activated it. Within a few minutes, the small tablet-screen showed a hot-spot near Madame Tussauds. "It's next door, in the basement of the Planetarium." Kyler exclaimed.

"Somehow, that seems appropriate," Tertia observed.

Kyler grabbed his tablet and stood. "Let's get there pronto."

Flashing their ID cards gained them access. The caretaker switched on the basement lights for them. Beneath the Planetarium was a massive store-room draped in cobwebs, the floor covered in dust. In a far corner was a replica of the Zygma projector in the theater. "We've struck gold," Kyler enthused.

With Tertia's assistance, Kyler hooked up his tablet to the projector and jabbed at a wireless keyboard, interrogating the system.

Finally, he exclaimed, "Look here." Kyler had switched the screenview to a spreadsheet record of time-jaunts. "He was methodical all right. See, he jumped a little earlier, to December 192 AD."

Tertia indicated the blank box on the right of the column. "But this suggests he hasn't returned yet."

"He's been gone sixteen months—our time." A cold fist clamped round his heart. "My precog dream." He groaned. "It could be the harbinger of massive change."

"Tell me about it," Tertia urged.

So he did.

IV

Kyler typed in the contact number for Sebastian Bulmer on his slimfone. It chirped and the image of a gray-haired woman appeared on the handheld screen. "Mrs. Bulmer speaking. Do I know you? What do you want?"

Kyler explained and then asked to talk with her husband.

"He's away—been gone a year or more now. You should know, he worked for Time Corps."

"A year or more, you say?" This confirmed the record all right.

"Yes," she snapped. "Have you lost him, then?"

She didn't seem perturbed.

"Haven't you been worried about his absence?" he asked.

She hunched her shoulders noncommittally. "We lead different lives. It suits us that way. He takes off for a year or so whenever he's writing another book."

"Have you got a picture of him?" Kyler asked.

"Yes." She jabbed at something off-view and instantly her image was replaced by a still of a bald man with a bushy white beard and moustache, dark brown eyes and protruding ears. "It's the most recent image I have of him. He uses it for publicity, more fool him; it's likely going to scare away potential readers, if you ask me."

With a swipe, Kyler transferred the Bulmer image to his slimfone. "Have you any notes he might have left regarding the book he's working on?"

"Yes. He doesn't like me going into his study, but if I didn't it'd be a foot thick of dust. I'll copy the details and send them."

"Thank you. I'll let you know when we locate him."

"That would be nice. We're overdue an anniversary dinner …"

Kyler closed the call.

* * *

"This is quite alarming," Sennacherib's chip-voice stated, bulbous black eyes roving over Tertia's chronovisor, another item she had procured from 'props.'

Kyler thought it made unsettling viewing. It was akin to those star-maps utilized with slimfones. Point the chronovisor at the street outside the window, and tap the backwards button and the screen showed in slow-mo the buildings from the past being demolished and rebuilt; tap the forward button and gradually the buildings altered, becoming shimmering Latinate edifices, yet indistinct. "The chronovisor suggests that these images are not firm yet. It is a *possible* future … not …"

"Not etched in stone yet?" Tertia said.

"Quite." Ensconced in his large Flexiglas tank, Sennacherib scanned the files on the flat-screen Kyler held up. "You both need to travel there and bring back Bulmer. We must hope that whatever he's doing hasn't yet altered time. Changing an actual alteration is exceedingly complex and fraught with difficulty."

"Even for you?" Kyler asked.

"Even for me."

"Weapons?" Kyler prompted.

"Lasers and knives only," Sennacherib advised. "Definitely no swords and no modern weapons or explosives. We've had to let go half of our recovery crew, so we must reduce the need for tidying up anachronisms."

Tertia gestured. "I can arrange that—the lasers and knives."

"From props again?" Kyler suggested with a grin.

* * *

Suitably attired in toga—"where are their pockets?"—with sandals and woolen socks, Kyler studied Tertia in her gold-trimmed white robes. "I think we need furs, it will be cold where we're going."

Tertia opened a chest and pulled from it two wolf-skin cloaks. "These will have to do. They're fake, of course, so won't be as efficient as the real thing."

"OK." He tapped behind his ear. "Have you got a linguachip?"

She smiled and put a finger to her temple. "Fully functioning."

He still found it weird. No matter what language his interlocutors used, the chip translated for him and also simultaneously translated his English as it left his lips into the lingua franca.

She told him he would use the name Manlius.

"You can't be serious? It's too close to manliness, and that sounds boastful."

"It has favorable antecedents, Kyler. Marcus Manlius Capitolinus was a Roman consul who saved Rome from the Gauls in the 4th century BC."

"Oh, in that case …. And what do I call you?"

"Tertia will suffice."

The notes received from Mrs. Bulmer were sketchy. It appeared that Bulmer was using the name Varius Rufinus. He'd also jotted down the name of Fabia, who was the wife of the governor of Britain, Clodius Albinus. "What does he want with her?" Kyler queried.

"I don't know." Tertia delved into her leather satchel and brought out a slim infopad. She tapped rapidly on its black surface. "She and her son were beheaded by Emperor Severus in 197 AD and thrown into the river."

At one time Kyler might have shuddered at that blunt statement. But in excess of two dozen jaunts into the past had inured him to the brutality of history. He was surprised how unaffected Tertia seemed.

"We'll definitely need these weapons, then," he said. He had a concealed pugio, the type of dagger used to assassinate Julius Caesar. Tertia kept her knife in the leather satchel with other "things" she didn't itemize for him.

The lasers resembled narrow wax tablets, but they were in fact formed from impervious plasmet compound; they could easily be concealed. Slight pressure on the appropriate incised glyph triggered the laser beam; its intensity could be adjusted by tapping a series of other glyphs.

Their individual recall beacons were fitted to their ankles in the guise of gold snake anklets.

Tertia produced a pair of fragile-looking careworn Roman leather shoes. "These are one pair of roughly two hundred found in Vindolanda, a frontier town near the Wall," she said. "One each; they'll serve as our focus objects."

"What's the period?"

"The same as Bulmer, December 192 AD," she replied, her free hand clasping his.

The Zygma projector's faceted lens spun, emitting shards of light in panoply of colors. Despite being accustomed to the process, Kyler still felt his stomach lurch as the machine increased its intensity. The shoes in their hands were pinned by the twin beams of two lamps on either side of the projector.

Slo-mo, he perceived their surroundings wobble, grow dim and seemingly cease to exist, as the time-shunt from now to then assaulted his every fiber of being, plunging him into disconcerting yet familiar darkness.

V

Although the sun shone weakly, Kyler shivered, despite the fake fur cloak, which wasn't surprising: they were in the great outdoors of northern Britain and the ground was covered in snow.

The sky was gray, with low-slung milky clouds threatening to deposit more white stuff.

Breath pluming from his mouth, he stood next to Tertia. Their backs were pressed against a stone and wood wall. He quickly realized it wasn't *the* Wall.

Tertia hastily shoved the two shoes into her capacious satchel.

They were in a town where people bustled about. Two oxen pulled a cart filled with wood, wheels converting the snow to muddy slush; women hefted wicker baskets; some men sat at tables in the portico opposite, wrapped in cloaks, quaffing drink. Several strip-houses opened onto the main thoroughfare, their sloping roofs revealing red tiles through patches of snow. A handful of stalls were erected, the sellers stamping their feet and blowing on their hands as they peddled their food and pottery wares. A blacksmith hammered at a horseshoe, while two children stood nearby, warming themselves. A man sat sewing leather into the form of a shoe; a couple of women gossiped on the corner. The strong smell of animal droppings and burned wood assailed his nostrils and he coughed.

Ironically, he looked forward to jumps into the past, because the air was fresh and not manufactured; yet whenever he found himself in a medieval or even an

Old West township, one of the first things that struck him was the stench—of human and animal waste, of animals themselves, and often the overpowering and stomach-churning stink from tanneries.

"Where are we?" Kyler whispered.

"It's the vicus—the civil settlement just south of the fort and the Wall."

"How do we go about finding Bulmer?"

"We ask—using this." From her satchel she held up an ink sketch of their quarry.

"How'd …?"

"Simple printing technique: scan then select sketch mode, and print on fake parchment; though this stuff won't crumple, crumble or tear."

They made for the nearest tavern, a wooden shack with a lopsided sign above the doorway, and entered. The floor was covered in straw. To the left was a stone hearth with flames cavorting round rough-hewn logs.

Six swarthy men sat at a makeshift bar area, flagons in their hands; they were the only customers.

A serving woman in a grimy thick woolen shift approached them. "We don't get many women in here," she said, smiling.

"A pity." Tertia gestured at the fireplace. "Nice place you've got, Miss …?"

"Beitris, ma'am." The woman glanced about her. "We hoped the fire would bring in more patrons on a day like this. You'll be wanting beer?"

"Yes," Kyler answered and led Tertia to a rickety table near the fireplace. Waves of warmth were comforting. Tertia placed her satchel on the table top and waited, retaining a hand under the leather flaps.

Beitris the serving woman brought their two flagons. Husks floated on the surface. Kyler took a sip: it was warm to the taste, so welcome, and chewy; he'd had worse in his travels.

Tertia flicked out the fake parchment and asked the woman, "Have you seen this man around here?"

Beitris stared at it, cocked her head. "Once, I think, but it was a while back. That's a good likeness. The artist has talent."

"He has. Anything else you can tell me?"

"He stayed at the mansio." Beitris thumbed behind her. "Preferred their fare to ours, I suppose. And they serve wine there."

One of the six men strolled over from the bar, his left eye covered by a leather patch. "Get about your business, Beitris, I want words with our guests."

Casting a fearful gaze on One-eye, Beitris scuttled away to the bar.

Leaning on the table, his face inches from Tertia's, One-eye said, "What's a pretty lassie doing with this fop, eh?"

"He's my husband," she replied equably.

"He isn't man enough for you, honey," One-eye grated, straightening. "I am." He clutched his crotch and gestured coarsely.

"I advise you to go away." Kyler lowered his flagon and wrapped his fingers around the concealed laser.

Turning to his mates, One-eye chuckled. "He's *advising* me!" Abruptly, he swung round, short knife drawn, its point resting against Kyler's chin. "Now, laddie, how about you leaving me and your missus alone for a while so we can get to know each other, eh?"

"Yes," Kyler croaked. That was the trouble when visiting the past: people could be so unpredictable. *One-eye could as easily have cut my throat*, he thought, mouth suddenly dry. "Have a care," he whispered hoarsely. "I'm going." He stood, keeping his hand in the folds of his robes.

"Sensible coward," One-eye growled.

The knife tip pricked Kyler's chin, drew blood.

Slickly, in one swift movement, Kyler pressed the incised activate glyph and swung the laser sword round and up, anxious not to castrate himself. The laser blade cut a portion of Kyler's robe and sliced off the man's arm at the elbow. There was very little blood as the beam had a cauterizing effect. The arm and the hand still clasping the knife hit the floor with a dull thud.

The other five charged, flinging tables and chairs aside; all of them held ugly curved knives.

Tertia brandished a knife from her satchel and jumped on a table, launching herself at the foremost two men. She didn't use her laser, just the knife, slitting the throat of the first man at once, pirouetting away and slicing into the second man's hamstring; he collapsed in a yelping heap and a third attacker tripped over him.

Kyler used a chair as a shield to thwart a downswipe from a knife, then thrust one of the wooden legs into the attacker's face. He left it impaled in the man's eye-socket and swung on his heel, using the laser blade to literally disarm another attacker. Blood was soaked up by the straw floor-covering.

"Let's get out," Tertia called to him.

Kyler needed no urging. Hastily deactivating and concealing his laser tablet, he darted for the doorway, Tertia snagging her satchel and instantly on his heels.

The cold air hit him as he emerged on the street.

VI

Turning left, they ran and covered two blocks, and then rounded a corner to face a door set into a white wall.

"In here," Tertia whispered, opening the door.

As Kyler shut the door behind them, they stood, panting, wisps of breath escaping. Tertia tugged him into the shadows of a portico and at her suggestion they hastily examined each other. Surprisingly, despite their brutal and bloody ordeal, their clothing wasn't too badly stained: a few specks of dried blood, but nothing to warrant questioning. "Blood-stains from sacrifices are not uncommon here," Tertia said. "We'll pass muster."

Kyler looked around. "What is this place?"

They stood at the entrance of a large courtyard. At the far end was a two-story dwelling, its walls white plaster. The courtyard was bordered on all sides by a veranda supported by wooden pillars.

"This is a mansio," she said.

"Mansio?"

"Beitris mentioned it. Where Bulmer's staying. It's a kind of hotel, where messengers, officials and officers stay. Like an inn."

"Better than a tavern, I hope," Kyler said ruefully.

She pointed to the two-story building. "That's probably reserved for visiting Imperial administrators, fiscal officers, investigators, special commissioners of military rank, complete with its own bath suite."

Garbed predominantly in blue and red clothing, several men and women were busy in the courtyard, carrying baskets of bread, pails of water and bundles of wood. None of them seemed to have noticed the abrupt arrival of potential guests.

A wooden door to their left was ajar. "In here," Tertia urged and slid inside.

Kyler followed.

Against the far wall was a latrine capable of taking eight sittings; a man and a woman were seated at present.

"Good day!" Tertia exclaimed and ushered Kyler out.

Wafting the air about his nose, Kyler pushed the next door along the veranda. "Let's try this one." He entered, Tertia close behind.

"It's unoccupied, a guest room," she observed.

The dimly lit place was about ten feet square and was furnished with a bed, a table, two chairs, and a sideboard. A single window overlooked the field and the great Wall beyond. The white plaster that covered Hadrian's Wall reflected the weak wintry sunlight.

Kyler reckoned the structure would be visible for miles—taunting the northern people.

"We still have a problem," he said. "How are we going to find Bulmer? Your parchment picture didn't help much."

Tertia chuckled and withdrew a small speckled ball from her robes.

"Something else from props?"

"It's a Zygma particle detector. Anyone who travels through the projector is bathed in an invisible yet distinctive bloom."

"Why bother with the parchment likeness of Bulmer, then?"

"Because if we'd met someone who knew him, we might glean from them more information about Bulmer's purpose."

Suitably rebuked, Kyler watched as she studied the ball.

Two of the ball's speckles lit up.

"But that could be us?"

"You're right. It is." Poking the tip of her tongue between her lips as she concentrated, she fingered the ball's underside and at once a third speckle lit up. A little more tinkering and the first two speckles darkened, leaving only the one shining. "It will glow green when we're in the vicinity of Bulmer."

Kyler shook his head in dismay. "Uncle Damon's never shown me one of those before."

"He probably hasn't used one yet."

"Yet?"

She smiled. "A slip of the tongue." From her satchel she produced a parchment map of the area, showing Hadrian's Wall, forts and settlements, and laid it flat on the table.

"You've come prepared, I see," Kyler observed.

"Part of my training." She slowly rolled the ball over the map and the speckle glowed brighter as it moved towards the marking that designated the Wall. She turned to Kyler. "I feel inclined to swear."

"Don't mind me. But why?"

"Bulmer's on the northern side of the fucking wall."

"Oh."

"You can say that again."

"Oh."

She sighed. "I didn't mean it literally!"

Kyler laughed. "No need to have a hissy fit. This isn't the first jaunt where the coordinates of arrival have been adrift." He gestured at the window. "We'll just have to go through that gate in the Wall."

"It isn't that simple. We're dressed as civilians and civilians aren't allowed close to the Wall. That's why there are no dwellings on the other side of the vallum ditch."

Becoming exasperated at her using yet another new term, he pointed sharply out the window. "And where's this ditch?"

"You can't see it from here, but you'd fall into it if you walked a short distance north in the dark. There are guarded earthen crossing points, of course. Further on you'll come across the military way, a typical Roman road that runs parallel with the Wall, and then the Wall itself. Then on the other side is another ditch for potential attackers to fall into."

"You seem to know a lot about this place."

"That's what being a Continuity girl entails, Kyler. It wouldn't do to get the ditches mixed up. The film would be spoiled and have to be ditched." Chuckling to herself, she turned to the door and added, "Let's go find Bulmer."

VII

As they emerged from the guest room, there was a commotion at the far end of the courtyard, at the doorway of the two-story building.

A tall Roman in expensive robes flung a woman to the ground.

Two legionaries bent to pick her up and held her between them. "What do you want us to do with her, Clodius Albinus," one of them said.

"Hold her still while I question her further."

"Please, dominus," the woman pleaded, "I know nothing!"

As ever, Kyler was grateful for the linguachip.

The Roman slapped her face twice; one of his gold rings scored her cheek, drew blood and a gasp. "Tell me where my wife and Varius Rufinus have run off to."

Varius Rufinus—Bulmer, Kyler gaped.

The woman shuddered. "If I knew, I would tell you."

"Governor Clodius Albinus!" Tertia exclaimed as the Roman was about to hit the woman again.

The Roman lowered his arm and swung round to face Kyler and Tertia. "Who shouts my name?"

"I know where your wife has gone," Tertia said, bowing her head briefly in deference to the man, her senior in rank and gender.

Clodius Albinus possessed an unusual white complexion. His fair hair was tightly curled, as were his beard and moustache. He had small, narrow blue eyes that seemed to burn with an unholy fire.

Kyler's throat went dry. Out of the corner of his mouth, he whispered, "What are you doing?"

She ignored him and addressed the governor of Britain. "My husband and I have been looking for Rufinus."

"And who might you be?"

"Manlius and Tertia," she said by way of introduction. "We have recently learned that Rufinus passed through the gate, going north with a wagon and an escort of auxiliaries."

"You saw them? When?"

"No, we didn't see them. But our source—who has gone now—said that Rufinus definitely went north."

Albinus cursed. "Then he must have taken Fabia with him." His brow creased and he glared at Tertia. "Why do you want Rufinus?"

"He owes money to my husband."

"Your husband doesn't seem very garrulous. He lets you do the talking, eh?" He winked.

"Women have gifted tongues," Kyler said, winking back.

Albinus chortled and then turned to the legionaries. "Get me Centurion Draco. I require an escort to go after my wife. And bring her handmaid with us."

Kyler took a pace forward. "May we accompany you, Governor?"

"Yes, I don't see why not. New faces, new life-stories to tell on the journey." He looked askance at Tertia. "Though I do wonder if it is wise to bring you along, my dear. It will be dangerous."

"I can look after myself, Governor," she said.

"I can vouch for that," Kyler added with feeling.

VIII

Their caravan consisted of two wagons. Tertia sat in the second beside the driver. Fabia's handmaiden had to walk beside it. A mount had been provided for Kyler. He was quite familiar with saddles that didn't have stirrups; not for the first time, he'd toyed with the idea of introducing them earlier than history allowed. There were two Roman cavalrymen in the van; in the rear on foot were eighty auxiliaries of Syrian and Spanish provenance. Albinus rode in the forward wagon, the mounted centurion Draco beside him. Four spare mounts were tethered to the rear of the wagons.

Before they set out, Albinus had explained that once they passed beyond the Wall they would first travel in a kind of buffer zone; a few miles ahead was the domain of the client chieftain, Drostan. "He's loyal to Rome."

"Good to know," Kyler had replied.

"But beyond, we will be prey to the Picts."

Not a comforting thought.

Now, as they passed the cemeteries on either side of the road, Kyler leaned towards Tertia and asked, "Can we talk?"

Tertia glanced at the wagon driver. "Don't worry, he's Algerian and doesn't understand us. The centurion gives him orders."

"Have you any idea what Bulmer's really doing here?" He eyed her leather satchel.

She chuckled. "It doesn't contain all the answers, Kyler. I can't believe he's eloped with Fabia to the Pictish north. It's far too dangerous. He's only doing research for a book, after all. There has to be another pressing reason for him going there."

"Whatever it is, it's highly likely it's going to affect history."

"That's the paradox, isn't it?" she mused. "We're still here, so presumably the past isn't too different if we exist, no?"

"You really think we might just blink out of existence if somebody tampers seriously with the past—our past?"

"I don't know. Finding witnesses would be hard, wouldn't it?"

Kyler laughed at the absurdity.

They passed the fort on their left and followed the road that bordered a burn in full flow with shards of ice floating on the roiling surface.

Crossing the vallum, they proceeded towards the milecastle and its gate.

Briefly, they stopped at the gate while Albinus conversed with the sentries, and then they were waved through the gateway.

As they passed beyond the Wall, Kyler sensed a transformation in the mood of the men marching nearby. Their faces appeared somber now; understandably, since before their departure the fort commander had advised Albinus against chasing after his wife. "You can get another wife, Governor, but you're only given one life. Besides, she's bestowed you with an heir in Cato."

What was Bulmer doing?

In a short while the Wall was behind them, and they passed a frozen wide lough bordered by reeds on their left.

They headed north, trudging in ankle-deep snow. Behind them was a dirty slushy mess, an obvious trail for any tracker to follow.

* * *

Before dark descended—as it would early this far north—Centurion Draco ordered the caravan to halt and make camp. He also organized sentries and sent scouts north.

Tents were erected on the banks of a meandering brook and meals were quickly prepared and served.

Kyler and Tertia were on their way to Albinus' tent, having been invited for a meal, when a trumpet blared, as if in alarm.

Kyler swung round but relaxed as Tertia touched his arm and whispered, "It's nothing to worry about. Chieftain Drostan has entered the encampment."

Now Kyler spotted the man, a giant of at least six feet six inches in height, with a red beard and moustache, crowned by a metal helm. He was accompanied by an entourage of twenty warriors, all clad in a variety of fur and plaid clothing.

Centurion Draco saluted and welcomed Drostan and then led him to Albinus who stood outside his tent, studying a map.

"I think we should listen to what is said," Tertia remarked. They both hurried to the tent as pleasantries were exchanged between Albinus and Drostan.

"It is an honor to meet you, Governor," Drostan was saying. "But I am concerned about your safety. My old acquaintance Centurion Draco tells me you seek your spouse in the company of a stranger."

"I do," Albinus said. "Have you news for me?"

"I met the lady Fabia on her way north."

"She was well?" Albinus asked anxiously.

"Yes. She was in the company of a man called Varius Rufinus and a Roman soldier by the name of Livius Macer."

Kyler was surprised to see Albinus' complexion paled even more.

"Macer?" Albinus queried. "You're sure?"

"Och, aye. I asked why they traveled without any guard. For only three to go north invited capture and death. They would not divulge their purpose and refused the aid I offered. It seems they had dismissed the auxiliaries soon after leaving the Wall."

"That tallies with what I have learned. I queried the guards on the gate about their departure. I could not understand how they were allowed to pass through," Albinus said. "The Roman who accompanied them hadn't given a name, but he was a man of authority and assured the sentries that his mission was urgent but safe."

Drostan grunted. "That may be so. But foolhardy."

"Governor, do you know Livius Macer?" Tertia asked.

Albinus seemed unsettled, clearly in a quandary. "I have heard of one such, but that was long ago—another time." He fingered his chin in thought. "An echo from the past."

"Chief Drostan, which way did they go?" Centurion Draco asked.

"You will need to keep to the northern road, until you come to an ancient bridge. My scouts watched the three of them cross it. It will be a full day's travel for your people to reach it."

"Will you join us in our quest, Chieftain Drostan?" Draco asked.

"Surely. I and the men I have brought will go as far as the bridge. But we will not cross it."

"Why not?" Albinus snapped.

"I cannot guarantee you will be safe if you go across."

Albinus' brow creased. "This is your territory, is it not, Drostan?"

Drostan gestured around him. "All this is within my influence. But beyond that bridge is not. None of our people would cross that bridge. Evil abides on the other side."

Albinus released a brief barking laugh. "Forgive me, but you are a great chieftain. Surely you are not afraid of a bridge?"

"I know no fear, Governor. But it is what lies beyond the bridge that troubles me and my people. I urge you not to cross."

Centurion Draco stepped forward. "I agree with Chieftain Drostan, sir."

Albinus shook his head. "I seek only my wife. Nothing more."

IX

The next day they broke camp and were accompanied by Drostan and his men. The chieftain's estimate was accurate and it was towards day's end, as the sun sank over the craggy horizon, when they determined on a halt.

A short way beyond was a wide brook gushing with meltwater spanned by a bridge made of stone and wood. Mist meandered above the watercourse and the narrow crossing.

"Hopefully the mist will dissipate on the morrow," Albinus said. "I don't fancy traveling in that murk, we'd be vulnerable to an ambush."

"We will leave you here, Governor," said Drostan and left with his men.

Camp was set up and darkness fell.

That night, Kyler and Tertia were guests of Clodius Albinus in his capacious tent.

Tertia enjoyed the honey biscuits and the partridge in aspic.

Fabia's maid served them wine and water.

"Is your son well?" Tertia enquired.

"Cato stays with the fort commander. He is anxious, concerned for his mother."

Kyler wondered if Bulmer's absconding with the governor of Britain's wife was sufficient cause to alter Albinus' future and perhaps the future of Rome—and even Britain. Pebbles thrown into ponds caused ripples, he knew; and there was the so-called "butterfly effect" to consider. Before any of the team had embarked on Continuity jumps, they'd been inculcated with the fact that by simply visiting another time continuum they were likely to alter in some small part that time-flow: the observer affected the experiment. "It is a risk we must take to avoid greater calamity," Sennacherib had stated.

Albinus turned to Kyler. "Now, tell me, why are you really intent on finding Varius Rufinus. And don't give me that nonsense about owing you money. I don't believe you would risk your lives beyond the Wall for a debt."

"You're right, Governor," Kyler replied, equably. "He is a fugitive and I'm an investigator sent to capture him." True enough, after a fashion.

"I wonder … Or did the Emperor Commodus send you to spy on me?"

"No. Why?"

"Oh, he and I have our differences."

Suddenly, there was a commotion outside the tent.

Albinus twisted in his chair, barked, "Sentry, what is it?"

Centurion Draco poked his head through the flap. "My apologies for disturbing you, sir. A man has come to speak with you."

"Show him in, then."

An elderly man stooped his head to step inside. His gray and white hair and beard were long and unkempt, his eyebrows bushy and thick. His eyes were deep-set in their sockets, yet glinted silver from the shadow created by the prominent brow. His nose was big and curved. He wore a long white robe tied with a belt of twined gold thread; at his hip was a sheathed knife, and fitted to his belt were three bulging leather pouches. Draped round his neck was a necklace of metal ornaments that jangled as he moved.

He posed no threat; Centurion Draco stood at his shoulder, hand on the hilt of his sword.

"I have come to speak with you, Clodius Albinus," the stranger said in a deep resonating voice.

"By the gods, who are you?" Albinus demanded.

"Cambion Ambrosius." He bowed his head slightly. "From the north and other points of the compass."

Albinus chuckled. "A mystic, eh? A druid?"

"Some term me as such. I come with news of several matters that affect you, Governor Albinus on this, the last day of the year."

Albinus gasped. "So it is. Well, druid, what news do you bring?"

"Your emperor Commodus has been slain."

Albinus jerked forward in his chair. "When, man? How can you know this?"

Centurion Draco drew his sword. "No messenger has arrived, sir."

"What nonsense do you speak, Ambrosius?" the governor demanded, leaning forward in his chair. "And have a care. My centurion's blade thirsts for fresh blood."

Ambrosius heaved his shoulders, and his necklace made a discordant musical sound. "I saw it in a vision. Commodus was poisoned by his mistress Marcia, but survived, so her fellow conspirators employed the emperor's wrestling partner Narcissus to strangle him in his bath."

"Narcissus? You know of him, yet surely this cannot be true."

"Sir," interrupted Centurion Draco, "shall I remove this fool?"

Ambrosius raised a hand, palm outwards, revealing blue esoteric tattoo markings. "My visions are never wrong, Governor."

Albinus stayed the centurion with a gesture and then eyed the druid. "But—but who will be emperor now?"

"Do you not desire that honor?" the druid asked.

"No, no …. But wait, you said 'news of several matters.' What other calamity do you wish to reveal?"

"It is not a calamity. I bring news of your spouse."

Albinus abruptly got to his feet. "If you come to ransom her, you will rue that decision, man. I'll torture the truth from you."

"She is unharmed. But her presence among our people is troublesome. We merely ask that you take her away."

Albinus let out a barking laugh. "Troublesome, eh? Yes, she can be that, right enough!"

Shrugging diplomatically, Ambrosius said, "I can direct you to her."

"Why didn't you bring her to me?"

"You must cross the bridge to see her. It is ordained."

"I intend to cross tomorrow with my men."

"No, Clodius Albinus, you cannot bring your soldiers. Only civilians are permitted to cross."

"Permitted?" Saliva drooled on Albinus' lips. "The might of Rome does not bow to your northern nonsense."

Ambrosius exhaled noisily. "Then you will not see your wife again." He turned to Kyler. "And the man you seek will also be beyond your reach forever."

Before Kyler could respond to this, Albinus swung round to face him and Tertia. "These two civilians will be by my side. Like me, they are armed and capable of fighting."

Kyler stared. "How—?"

Albinus sneered. "Nothing transpires within my orbit without me knowing of it. You both acquitted yourselves well in that tavern." He pointed to the few dried blood spots on Kyler's robes.

Centurion Draco cleared his throat. "If I resign and become a civilian, sir, I could join you."

"No, Centurion. I respect your loyalty. But you are needed to stay here, with your men. I may require you and them on our return."

"Very well, sir." The centurion clasped the governor's hand and forearm. "Let it be so written."

Reassured by the knowledge that the recall beacon's button was around his ankle, Kyler nodded. "We'd be glad to go with you, Governor."

"No, not you," Albinus said, waving away Tertia. "It is too grave a risk for a woman."

Tertia stood arms akimbo and said forcefully, "I should think that your wife would welcome female company in this stressful time, Governor."

"Very well." He was certainly quick to make a decision. Now, he eyed the druid. "I will cross the bridge with these two."

"That *is* permitted," said Ambrosius with no hint of irony.

Kyler realized that the centurion probably feared that the governor of Britain was going to his death and he would be punished for letting it happen. Yet according to the history Tertia had divulged, Albinus would live on for another four years or so; unless the events set in train by Bulmer had already affected the future, and Albinus was destined to die much sooner. Despite the safety-valve of the recall beacon, Kyler felt a chill trail his spine at the prospect of being in a life-or-death situation alongside the governor of Britain. The presence of Tertia comforted him a little.

"How did you get here?" Albinus enquired of the druid.

"The mist aided me, Governor."

"And will you accompany us across the bridge?"

"No. I will see you at the other side. I will leave you now to enjoy the remainder of your meal." Bowing slightly, Ambrosius pivoted on his heel and ducked through the tent flap.

Kyler jumped from his chair and followed, peering out the opening.

The camp was doused in a fine drizzly mist. Globules of moisture on the tents and the ground shone eerily in the moonlight. The vague shape of the druid strode along between lines of tents for a few feet and then vanished into the murk.

X

The mist of last night had lifted and the bridge was in plain view. Beyond, on the other side of the brook, the land seemed insubstantial, as if viewed through warped glass. Armed auxiliaries guarded the bridge on this side. Kyler strolled to the bank of the brook. The ground cracked under his feet, the frost crisp, reflecting scintillating shards of light bestowed by the morning sun.

Centurion Draco ordered three saddled horses to be brought forward. He saluted the governor. "The backpacks contain blankets, a sword, flint and food to last three days, sir."

"If we have not returned in three days, Centurion, you can return to Vindolanda and ask Rome to dispatch a new governor."

Draco shook his head. "If you do not return in that time, sir, I will cross the bridge with some of my men and find you."

"Gratitude for your loyalty." He mounted his horse and returned the centurion's salute.

Tertia and Kyler swung into their saddles, and all three rode towards the bridge.

As they trotted up the slight incline of the crossing, Kyler said, "You seem comfortable in the saddle, Tertia. Have you ridden before?"

"Many times—with the emphasis on 'times,'" she replied with a grin.

Riding the slight down-slope on the other side, they passed a couple of staffs planted in the ground, their attached cross-pieces adorned with effigies and metal ornaments.

"Pay it no heed," Albinus said. "Druid nonsense, that's all."

They had been riding along a road churned by cartwheels for some time when Kyler spotted on their right a half-demolished round-house made of rough-hewn stone. Wary, he rode over to it, but it was empty. It might have been a fortification in the past, but now it was crumbling, though a section of it offered adequate shelter from the elements.

"Your caution does you credit, young man," Albinus said. "These brochs are ancient, I've been told."

"I'm worried about an ambush, Governor. I'm not too sure we should have trusted Ambrosius."

"We had no choice," Tertia said.

Some miles later, Kyler observed ahead a plume of black smoke rising from behind a hill.

"Take care. Follow me." Albinus urged his horse into a lope and rode up the hillside.

When Kyler and Tertia joined him on the crest, all their horses snorted and whinnied. Perhaps distressed at the smell rather than the sight.

On another hill a few hundred yards away was a wicker effigy in the shape of a giant man. It had been set alight moments earlier, it seemed, and smoke spiraled into the wintry sky. Tethered within the wicker effigy was a bald, naked man. He screamed in agony as flames licked at his feet.

About thirty people dressed in furs clustered round the bonfire, shouting and cheering. On a boulder to their right stood a woman, her fur cloak billowing behind her, her gray hair streaming in the breeze. Draped round her neck was a necklace of animal teeth and metal trinkets. Her words carried to them on the wind: "Death to evil wizards!"

Kyler edged his horse forward, his mouth suddenly very dry.

Tertia whispered, "Isn't that—?"

"They're sacrificing Varius Rufinus," Albinus exclaimed. "By Mithras, if they have harmed Fabia …" He rammed his heels into the side of his horse.

As the three of them rode towards the flank of the howling mob, Tertia said, "We're too late."

37

Already, one side of Bulmer's face and body was scorched.

Men with woad-painted faces rushed forward and grabbed at the reins of their horses.

Kyler scanned the mob. There was no sign of any Roman woman in distress; and there wasn't another wicker effigy, or even the burnt remains of one.

Albinus kicked away two men and urged his horse to the side of the boulder. He growled at the woman, "Why do you sacrifice this man?"

"What business is it of yours, Roman?"

She was short in stature, her shoulders stooped, her face daubed in blue. Her nose was flat and skewed, as if broken. Her dark pebble-eyes glinted under a prominent brow. Thin lips curling in disgust, she snapped, "Take them to the village."

"There are too many," Kyler called to Albinus, who was about to draw his sword. "Think of your wife. We must find her."

Giving a reluctant nod, the governor allowed his horse to be led with the others.

The druid woman was given a horse and rode on ahead, singing as she went. Six huge warriors accompanied her on their own mounts.

Kyler peered over his shoulder.

Sebastian Bulmer was now slumped forward, still suspended by tethers, but he was unmoving. Flames cavorted up his frame, flesh bubbling. He was probably dead from smoke inhalation—or intense shock to his system. Glancing at Tertia, Kyler said, "I don't know how we're going to manage it, but we've got to retrieve his corpse. Recovery later might prove impossible."

"You're right. I've checked Bulmer's medical records."

"How'd you do that?" He eyed her satchel.

"Before we set off, I accessed the databank. His left shin has a metal pin in it, the surgery a result of a childhood accident, and he has four fillings in his teeth. They won't burn, even if the rest of him does." *Something to confound a future archaeologist.*

"What's the village they're taking us to?"

Tertia shrugged. "It isn't on any map, which shouldn't come as a surprise."

XI

Soon, they were able to see their destination; the village was spread out on the northern slope of the snowy hillside of a valley. Through the cleft in the earth meandered a stream, the ice broken at the water's edge beside the dwellings. The houses were all single-story, the roofs covered in thatch, the walls constructed with stone and mud. "Welcome to Gadoon," said one of their captors.

They descended to the village and were met by a motley collection of people, a number of them in timeworn accoutrements of Roman legionaries, others in Pictish attire, and many in plaid and wool. Men and women stared, curious, but kept silent.

The horses of all three of them were brought to a halt outside the largest hut. They were hauled off their mounts and thrust to the cold hard ground.

Villagers surrounded them, several glaring, grunting and scowling yet none offered any threatening gesture or brandished a weapon.

Abruptly, the crowd parted and the short hunched female druid emerged from the hut's doorway.

Albinus struggled to his feet. "What is the meaning of that?" he snapped, gesturing to the hill where smoke still spiraled.

"He was evil. He talked into a strange craft and it talked back to him."

"You utter nonsense," Albinus snapped.

She sneered. "I utter what the gods decide. We will all gain power from his sacrifice."

"Who are you?" Albinus demanded. "Where is Ambrosius?"

"I am Druidess Dornoll. Once the mate of Ambrosius." She scowled at mention of the druid's name. "He has been banished from Gadoon by the will of the people." She spun to face the crowd. "Take them to the holding hut for now, until we decide how their fate will appease the gods."

The press of numbers was too great, Kyler realized.

"Resistance is futile, indeed," Tertia said with a curl of her lips.

Half-dragged, half-walking, the three of them made their way past a number of huts and were then pushed towards a dark building with a solid oak door.

They were shoved inside, thrown to the floor, and the door was slammed shut.

A candle illumined the place, a single room.

Nursing his bruises, Kyler sat up. His eyes quickly adjusted to the shadowy interior.

Sitting on the far side of the room was a woman and a Roman soldier, both of them in their thirties or possibly forties. Their clothing was ripped in places.

"Fabia!" Albinus exclaimed, rushing to her side.

She got to her feet and they embraced awkwardly. Then they disengaged and she gestured to the Roman soldier. "My husband, meet Livius Macer, my cousin."

Albinus stared. "It can't be. He was in the Ninth Legion."

"The same," said the soldier.

"But the legion was lost over seventy years ago. You'd be in your nineties, at least."

"That is correct, Albinus. Your wife has told me all about you."

"You must explain," Fabia said.

"Very well, cousin. We left York in pursuit of a large band of Brigantes. The running battle raged for days and weeks, always moving north. Hadrian's Wall wasn't built then, though I have heard of it and visited there twice in the last decade or so. But I get ahead of myself. We fought to a standstill at the Gadoon Bridge."

"Ah, the bridge …" mused Tertia.

Livius looked askance at her, puzzled, and then went on, "A druid appeared out of the mist. Ambrosius, he called himself."

"We've met him," said Kyler.

"Oh, is he well?"

"The last we saw of him, yes."

"I feared Dornoll might have taken his life. It is good that he yet lives. Well, Ambrosius urged us to cross the bridge together to heal our wounds. I still don't know why, but as soon as we set foot on the other side of the bridge we all felt exceedingly weary of fighting. We came to this village of Gadoon and buried our differences. The valley has that effect, it seems … We have been here ever since, sharing it with the original Picts and the Brigantes, guided by the druid Cambion Ambrosius."

"But you've barely aged," Albinus exclaimed.

"The valley itself is mystical in some way. The charm works on us so long as we stay."

Kyler turned to Fabia. "Why did Varius Rufinus bring you here?"

"He explained that he had done a lot of research on ancient tablets. I didn't understand that, I must admit. He said he'd learned that my cousin Livius was still alive and near the town of Vindolanda."

Livius took up his explanation again. "Everything had been all right. We all accepted our lot and made new lives here in the valley. But then Ambrosius became enchanted by the woman Dornoll. Over time, she bewitched him and soured the populace against him. I slipped away and went to the Wall, hoping to recruit troops to bring back to restore order …"

"And you met Varius, is that it?" Tertia interrupted.

Livius nodded. "Yes. And when he introduced me to Fabia, a cousin, I was surprised. And pleased." He grasped Fabia's hand briefly. "Have you seen him? Is he all right?"

Kyler pursed his lips and then said, "I regret that he is dead. Dornoll sacrificed him."

Livius swore and grated his teeth. "The bitch!" His eyes clouded. "What of Ambrosius, when did you last see him?"

"A day ago, I think, he appeared out of the mist at my camp," Albinus said. "We haven't seen him since."

"You have men at your camp?"

"Yes. But Ambrosius warns that they should not cross the bridge."

Livius nodded. "The arch druid is right. Anyone who comes to this valley will be subject to the longevity charm. If too many people came from outside the valley, the charm would be broken."

"Who says?" Kyler asked.

"I do," said Ambrosius, standing in the doorway, leaning on his staff. Mist meandered around him and dissipated at his sandaled feet.

Livius gave a short laugh. "I'm glad to see you, old friend! But what about Dornoll?"

Ambrosius scowled. "She is talking with her clansmen, debating who to sacrifice next to mediate between the village people and our gods. I fear it will be you, Livius. She will not be satisfied by simply observing the flight and calls of birds and by the sacrifice of holy animals. She seeks to demolish the valley's charm. The wicker man sacrifice is one way.

She will now resort to a more intimate human sacrifice, plunging a dagger into your chest. By observing the way your limbs convulse as you succumb and the gushing of your blood, she maintains she will be able to read the future."

"That's barbaric," Fabia exclaimed.

"No worse than what Rome does, I fear," said Tertia.

Fabia lanced a glare at her.

"But Ambrosius," Livius said, "Can't you fight her and gain the backing of the village folk?"

"I might—with the help of you two," the druid said, pointing at Kyler and Tertia. "They took the governor's sword but didn't relieve you of your belongings, I see."

Tertia grinned knowingly.

"What do we do now, then?" Kyler asked.

XII

Kyler exited the hut first. The single sentry stared, disbelief on his face, and then raised his spear to thrust at Kyler's stomach. As taught by Melody, their aikido instructor, he stepped to the side, grabbed the spear haft with both hands and thrust up his right elbow into the sentry's throat, while continuing to turn; a perfect *jotori*, he reckoned. As the sentry let go of the spear, Kyler discarded it and swiftly sliced the edge of his hand—executing a *yokomenuchi* move—to the side of the man's neck before he could utter a sound. The sentry fell to the ground, unconscious.

Tertia emerged by his side and Ambrosius bent to retrieve the fallen spear.

"Stay here," Tertia told Albinus and Fabia.

The three of them strode over the frost-covered ground, footsteps crunching. As they approached the main hut, several villagers noticed them and huddled in their doorways, watching. A few men moved forward, hands gripping clubs, spears or knives.

Ambrosius eyed them. "This is between me and Dornoll," he boomed.

The menacing men faltered.

Kyler took out his laser, activated its blade; it made a faint sizzling sound. The watchers heard it and backed away. He heard one of them wheeze, "More dark magic!"

What had Bulmer been doing?

Ambrosius came to a halt outside the big hut. Dornoll emerged from the doorway, followed by six broad husky men carrying short-swords.

"I banished you from the village, Ambrosius. You were foolish to return." She pointed at Kyler and Tertia. "They are my prisoners and will be sacrificed to remove the dark magic from this valley."

"The darkness comes from your base heart, Dornoll, not from these strangers. You killed Varius Rufinus in vain."

Dornoll cackled, revealing teeth filed to sharp points. She signaled to the men on either side of her.

Without a word, the six men stepped forward, wielding their swords.

Over his shoulder, Ambrosius said, "You spared that sentry, but don't spare any of these. They won't hesitate to kill you." And he rushed forward, thrusting the spear point into the foremost attacker's throat. As the dead man remained impaled, Ambrosius relieved him of his sword and swung round, cutting at another.

Kyler deflected a downward swipe of an attacker's blade. An instant later, the laser cut the blade in half and the man stared, disbelieving. Kyler followed through, the laser beheading him.

He heard Tertia yelling like a banshee but was too occupied with another swordsman to see what she was doing. He hoped she was all right.

The next assailant fared no better, his sword broken and his chest opened up to the breast-bone with the laser.

Kyler glanced over his shoulder, noting that Tertia stood atop two corpses and was fencing with a third man. A few inches away from Tertia, Ambrosius was battling with Dornoll, spear to spear, thrusting and countering. Then Tertia disarmed her assailant and sent him to meet his pagan gods. In the same instant, Dornoll let out an eldritch shriek as Ambrosius' spear point entered her chest. As if in a reflex action, she shoved her spear at Tertia, and it pierced her side.

"Tertia!" Kyler exclaimed and ran to her as she sank on top of the three corpses.

She was covered in blood, but most of it wasn't hers, he realized. Crimson oozed from her side. He grabbed folds of her robes and pressed the material against the wound. "We must activate the recall beacon, get you medical aid," he whispered.

She gripped his arm. "No, we can't leave yet."

"But it's over. Bulmer is dead; he can't do any harm to the timeline now."

"Before you go, you must retrieve his teeth and that metal pin," she told him.

"You're bleeding!"

"It will stop soon. Help me to my feet." She shuddered, expressing a great sigh. "I don't believe that Bulmer is the cause of what your vision revealed. We've missed something."

"But …"

"I'll mend, dear Kyler. We need to finish what we came to do."

Despairingly, he looked at Ambrosius. "You wanted us to cross the bridge so you could take back the valley, is that it?"

"Yes. Despite Dornoll's black arts and sacrifices, the charm is still active. Though I suspect I will have to conceal this valley from prying eyes in future." He stroked his beard. "Perhaps Gadoon can reappear from time to time, to admit the occasional stranger, to supply new blood."

"You used us."

"If you hadn't crossed the bridge, you would not have found the man you seek—Bulmer, as you call him. Now, we both have what we desire."

Ambrosius knelt at Tertia's side. He opened a leather pouch at his belt, removed a handful of fine herbs, and then sprinkled them on Tertia's wound. "It will help the healing." He pointed to Fabia and Albinus who were walking unsteadily towards them. "You must return them to Vindolanda so they can accomplish what they must." There was sadness in his eyes.

Kyler wondered if the druid had knowledge of the future. The lives of both Albinus and his wife had been saved, but their grim fate was still sealed in the annals of history.

XIII

Standing outside the long hut, Livius bid Fabia farewell. "It was good to see blood-kin after all these years."

"Return with us," she pleaded. "We will be going to Rome soon."

"No, my place is here with my men. The world has turned long since we were part of it. I wish you well, dear cousin."

Kyler and Tertia rode their horses, while a third mount was provided for Albinus and his wife. They made their way towards the hill top where the burnt remains of the wicker man and Bulmer smoldered.

While the Roman couple sat on their horse and watched in bewilderment, Kyler used his laser to cut loose the teeth and jaw-bone of the burnt skull and inserted it in a leather bag Ambrosius had supplied. Tertia sifted amidst the remnants of skeleton and retrieved the metal pin. It took a little longer to locate Bulmer's slimfone. It was shattered beyond repair, yet it was possible its chip might provide clues; perhaps some of Bulmer's dictation could be recovered in time. He remembered Dornoll's words: *He talked into a strange craft and it talked back to him.* Bulmer must have used his slimfone as a recorder, to make notes for his book.

Shaking off ash from their feet, they mounted their horses and made for the bridge.

On the way, Kyler asked Tertia, "How are you feeling now?"

"Sore. Weary. But I'll survive."

"Good. Glad to hear it. I was worried back there."

"Thanks for the concern, Kyler."

"In the village, you said we've missed something. What did you mean?"

"I can understand Bulmer investigating the clues concerning the missing Ninth Legion, and using Fabia to that end. But I can't see how her 'abduction' could alter history so severely."

"It's a bit of a stretch, granted. But if Albinus came after her, as he has done, then that would change things, wouldn't it? If he'd died at the hands of Dornoll, for example, he'd no longer be one of the five emperors."

"Yes, that's possible." She smiled. "But we were the ones who directed him to her possible whereabouts, on this side of the Wall, not Bulmer."

"Observers affecting the experiment, eh?"

"Let's hope not! That would mean that every time-jaunt would have detrimental effects, no matter how much corrective action was taken."

"Paradoxes piled upon paradoxes …"

Mist amassed on the ground, meandering over the frozen earth. The sky lowered, closing in on them. "I don't think we'll make the bridge before it gets dark," Kyler said.

"We'll find shelter for the night."

A short while later, they rode up to the dilapidated broch they'd passed on their journey north.

"This will do," Kyler said. "We can take turns at keeping watch."

"Still cautious?" Albinus said.

"I'll feel happier when we rejoin Centurion Draco, Governor. I won't settle until then."

It started to rain sleet, slanting down, lowering the ambient temperature. They were glad of the remains of a stone roof. They led the horses into a sheltered section and tethered them but at Tertia's suggestion they kept the animals saddled: "If we have to leave in a hurry," she explained.

Despite her wound, Tertia gathered bracken and twigs to build a fire and then lit it, surreptitiously using an implement from her satchel.

The night fell and as light departed the bitter cold increased. A north-easterly wind lashed at the stone, keening, as though the ghosts of the many fallen warriors here took exception to the new occupants. The unsettling sound was accompanied by occasional howls from wolves.

Firelight flickered, glowing on the walls of the broch. Kyler watched as Albinus used his knife to carve an inscription in a large stone that had tumbled from the wall: "To Jupiter, Best and Greatest, I Clodius Albinus,

Governor of Britain, offer gratitude for saving my beloved Fabia."

The governor's wife read it and wept, clasping his hand. "I'm sorry I caused you distress and put you in danger, my husband. Livius was very persuasive."

"He probably carried the valley charm with him, to enchant you away from my side."

Kyler's stomach churned. He felt awful, but it wasn't simply the lack of food. Oblivious of their fate, this married couple evoked kindness and love. Yet Tertia had said that history decreed Albinus was a severe and cruel commander. Did those traits only manifest themselves when he was on a campaign? Or would they appear later, during the conflict to gain the reins of power in Rome?

He whispered to Tertia, "I wish you hadn't told me of their fate."

When contesting for position of emperor, Albinus was defeated, captured and executed on the orders of Severus. In public view, Severus had Albinus' naked body laid out on the ground and rode his horse over it. He then beheaded Albinus and his wife and child. Albinus' headless body was thrown into the Rhône, together with the corpses of his murdered family. Severus sent the head to Rome to dissuade any other contender.

"I wish we could change some things, Kyler," she replied, "but we cannot."

XIV

Later, Kyler was roused from sleep: it was his turn to take the watch from Tertia. "All quiet," she whispered, and kissed him lightly, unexpectedly on the cheek.

"What was that for?" he said.

"For being there for me." She turned her back and walked to the far side of the room, to lie next to Fabia who huddled up to Albinus; the governor lay on his back, snoring, the inscribed stone close by.

In the early hours, as light etched across the skyline, Kyler heard something unmistakable; it was similar to the sound of the wagons as they traversed the snow-laden land on their way to Gadoon Bridge. He stood, sensing his limbs ache; the night's cold had seeped into his bones.

He moved to the broken wall, suddenly exposed and assailed by the cold air that wafted about. Clumps of snow had frozen on top of the stone. He peered out, surprised at how light the land seemed—due to the luminous quality of the snow, perhaps.

Out of the corner of his eye, he noticed movement to his right.

A shadow.

Stealthy.

He listened intently but heard nothing except the low moan of the air whispering over ancient stone.

Kyler held his breath as the gun barrel of a very modern weapon poked through the gap in the wall. It was aimed at the sleeping forms of Albinus and wife.

Without pausing to think, he grabbed at the barrel, jerking it to the left of its target at the instant that the weapon fired.

A bright blue glare swamped the interior, fleetingly illuminating the sleeping couple, Tertia and the tethered horses. A chunk of the inscribed stone near Albinus' head broke off and fell onto the ground amidst rubble. The horses whinnied.

As the weapon discharged, Kyler yanked hard at the barrel, pulling it out of the attacker's hand. Kyler flung the gun to the ground and swung round to face the intruder.

But all he saw was a hulking dark shape in furs hurrying down the slope towards a two-wheeled chariot hitched to two black horses. Swinging round, he ran to the tethered horses.

Tertia was awake now, her laser knife shining. Remarkably, Albinus and his wife still slept.

Kyler untethered his horse and jumped into the saddle. "I'll be back," he promised her, wheeling the animal round and giving chase.

The false dawn lent an eerie wan aspect to the countryside, faint pink light reflecting off the virgin snow. And like an ugly scar blemishing the whiteness was the trail left by the fleeing chariot.

Cold air battered him as he leaned forward on the horse's mane, digging his heels in, urging the animal to greater speed.

Dawn rushed across the landscape, faint weak sunlight painting the stark terrain of grass tussocks, rocks and boulders jutting through swathes of snowdrift.

Kyler seemed to be gaining, since the chariot's wheels met resistance, slewing left and right on the frozen rutted ground.

The charioteer peered over his shoulder as Kyler's horse drew closer.

The man had a dark complexion, his features drawn and narrow, beset with a straggly black beard.

"Stop, damn you," Kyler called in contemporary Anglic, sure that the man was from his own time. How else would he be in possession of an advanced weapon? Admittedly, Kyler wasn't an expert on weaponry, but he'd never seen or heard of a gun like that. Some kind of energy pulse, he guessed; it wouldn't leave any anachronistic trace, either. More powerful than a laser, too.

His horse was alongside the chariot now.

The wheels churned up mud, pebbles and clumps of grass clogged with ice and snow.

Kyler heaved himself to one side and thrust himself off his horse, jumping awkwardly over the waist-high side onto the chariot's floor. He tumbled into the man's legs.

Without letting go of the reins, the charioteer kicked out, landing a lucky heel against Kyler's shoulder. When the next kick was delivered, however, Kyler locked his arm on the man's calf and rolled his weight against him, forcing the man onto his knees.

The reins were dropped, but the team of horses carried on running.

Jouncing on the uneven ground, the floor beneath the pair lifted and fell, juddering. A sudden bounce disengaged them and the charioteer landed on Kyler's back, driving him to the floor. The man's knees pressed on Kyler's arms while he gained a chokehold. Mere inches away, Kyler saw the speeding churned track. The man pushed his face over the edge of the chariot floor, trying to force his head onto the unforgiving ground.

Another bounce and this time Kyler freed his right arm and scrabbled frantically in the pocket of his robes. He blindly activated the laser, and the blade of heat sliced upwards, searing the man's shoulders.

The man yelled in pain and the chokehold on Kyler's throat relaxed.

Kyler pocketed the laser and snatched a couple of fingers, twisting them, breaking them.

Perhaps a toughened Roman legionary or charioteer might have accepted the pain, but the assassin from the future wasn't made of such staunch stuff. Clutching his broken fingers, he sank back on the floor, and leaned against the side.

An instant later, the left wheel collided with a huge half-buried stone. The chariot slewed to the right, tottered while still being dragged on one wheel, and then the weight of the passengers and the chariot shattered the load-bearing wheel. Spokes flew everywhere and the floor was dragged bone-jarringly across the ground.

Kyler rolled off the floor and hit an area of frosted turf, knocking the wind out of him. By the time his momentum brought him to rest against a large boulder, he felt sure that every part of his body was bruised. He hastily examined his limbs and chest. All in one piece, though he'd suffered several cuts and one of his knees was bleeding. Specks of blood contrasted with the glinting white snow.

Supporting himself on the boulder, he regained his feet. But as soon as he put weight on his right foot, acute pain stabbed into his vitals. The leg wasn't broken, he reckoned, but his heel was seriously hurt, maybe fractured.

The charioteer had been thrown clear of the busted conveyance. The two horses stood some distance away, still hitched to the shaft.

Gritting his teeth, Kyler limped to the prostrate charioteer. Every step was agony and brought sweat to his brow.

Finally, he stopped and the pain was reduced to a nagging ache. He knelt by the man, and noted the burned shoulder, material fused to the flesh. He turned him over. The man's face was laced with fine cuts, and his shoulder and left arm were covered in blood. His chest heaved, so he was alive. Then, disconcertingly, he opened his dark eyes and lanced Kyler with a penetrating gaze. "You're a time traveler as well?" he wheezed incredulously.

"Yes, I am, damn you!" Kyler replied.

"Who in blazes are you and why'd you stop me?"

"I'm Kyler Knightly, field agent of Continuity Inc., an organization specifically created to stop people like you from trying to change history, you fool!"

"I'm no fool! My name is Pedro Niger. You won't have heard of me, because I'm not from your timeline."

This was getting absurd. "Different timeline? What do you mean?"

"I'm from *your* future, Kyler."

Before Kyler could respond, he was distracted by the two horses whinnying in distress, noisily dragging the chariot shaft with them.

Silver-gray shapes darted behind rocks.

Snarls reached him from concealment.

A howl went up, and another, more chilling than the freezing air.

Wolves.

And they'd scented blood.

XV

"Help me up, will you?" Niger pleaded.

Reluctantly, Kyler offered the man his hand.

Heaving Niger to his feet, Kyler said, "Have you got a weapon, a sword?"

"No, I only came with the Pulser." Niger moaned. "And you discarded that."

"Here, use this." Kyler handed Niger his knife and then checked his robes and located the laser.

"You expect me to fight wolves with this puny weapon?" Niger demanded.

"I expect you to protect yourself with it. I'll do the fighting with this." He activated the glyph and the laser blade extended its full length and shone.

Niger whooped. "That's more like it."

"Here they come," Kyler said.

The pack consisted of at least five wolves. Two moved towards Kyler and Niger on either side, while the fifth one approached from the front, its hackles up, head lowered, snarling, yellowed teeth drooling.

"Pack discipline," Kyler observed. "Pincer movement. Roman tactics," he ended, almost admiringly.

Then the advancing wolf launched himself at Kyler, vicious teeth bared.

Kyler slashed up and left and right with the laser blade and the animal splattered blood in every direction, several sections of its anatomy dully slapping to the ground.

But the others, two on either side, had launched their attack simultaneously, and jaws closed on Kyler's right bicep. Despite the intense pain, he skewered the creature with the laser blade.

The second one barged into Kyler's side, its jaws missing limbs as he'd swiveled and dealt with the jaws clamped to his arm. Sprawling on the ground, Kyler swung the laser round but abruptly the light-beam fizzled and went out. Damn! It had lost all power. It was supposed to recharge with sunlight, but there was precious little of that here in the wintry north.

Without the laser, he resorted to viciously slamming his fist wrapped around the useless laser-wax tablet against the wolf's nose. The beast backed off, yelping.

Rising to his knees, Kyler saw Niger sink his knife blade into the throat of a wolf on top of him, its slavering jaws inches from his face. The other wolf had its mouth clamped to Niger's left leg, worrying it.

More wolf howls erupted and Kyler's heart sank.

Limping to the partly demolished chariot, Kyler grabbed a splintered section of the floor and slammed it hard against the head of the wolf making a meal of Niger's leg. He drew blood and hit the animal again and again.

"Hey, you can stop," Niger shouted, "the poor animal's dead."

Dropping the bloody chunk of wood to the ground, Kyler twisted round and stared at Niger. "*Poor animal?*"

"They're hungry. They hunt for meat. That's what they do."

"Yeah, I suppose you're right. And I kill if I need to so I can survive."

On a rise ahead of them mustered five more wolves. These seemed younger and slightly smaller. But the combined tooth-power suggested they were as deadly as those who'd been vanquished.

Suddenly, the wolves pricked up their ears and then scattered, disappearing in the landscape within seconds.

A moment later, Tertia galloped towards them with Albinus and Fabia.

"The cavalry has arrived," Kyler exclaimed.

"Who is that?" Albinus asked, pointing to Niger.

"He's one of us," Tertia said. She pointed directly ahead, to the south. "Governor, ride that way for about an hour and you will come to Gadoon Bridge. Centurion Draco should still be waiting for you."

"You're staying here, this side of the Wall?" Fabia asked.

"For a short while. Now, go, and you will be safe."

"Gratitude for your help," Albinus said, bowing to Tertia and then Kyler. Then he heeled his horse and rode south with his wife.

Tertia dismounted and ran to Kyler's side. "Your arm, you've been bitten."

"It will mend," he replied with a grimace. He nodded at Niger. "His leg's been badly mangled."

Tertia eyed Niger and then strode to the wrecked chariot. She knelt and found a leather sack. Rummaging inside, she stared at Niger. "Are you going to explain why you're here?" She lifted up a chunk of an inscribed stone.

Kyler stared. "But that's—"

"Exactly." Tertia nodded. "This is the stone Albinus inscribed last night. Our new friend used it as a focus object to bring him here."

"His name's Pedro Niger," Kyler said, "and he came to kill Albinus."

Niger sneered. "I had to try. It is family honor."

"But you failed," Kyler said.

"Yes, I did."

"So why didn't you activate your recall beacon and return to your timeline?"

Tertia showed a gold amulet in her palm. "Because it was in this sack and you chased him so closely he didn't have time to get it to trigger the recall."

"What are you going to do with me now?" Niger demanded. "If you imprison me in your timeline, you'll affect my history."

Tertia nodded. "Tell us what we need to know, first. Then we'll decide what to do with you."

* * *

Pedro explained that he was a very distant relative of Pescennius Niger.

"That was one of those five emperors," Kyler interjected.

"Just let him tell us without interruption, Kyler," Tertia berated, tenderly bandaging his arm.

After Commodus was assassinated, Pertinax declared himself emperor, but he only lasted three months before being murdered. There was clamor from Albinus' troops for him to succeed as emperor.

Following Pertinax's murder, the position of emperor was auctioned off to Didius Julianus, since he could actually pay the troops. Learning of the Roman populace's displeasure at Julianus' accession, Niger, Albinus and Severus withheld their support for Julianus; each of them had legions behind them; Niger was highly regarded in Rome and he had the backing of the eastern legions, but he wasn't in Rome, and Severus soon was; Severus made his claim to be emperor, and obtained the support of Albinus and sent legions to hunt Niger. After several defeats with Severus and his legions, Niger was decisively beaten and captured while attempting to flee. He was beheaded, and his head was eventually displayed in Rome. After his victory in the east, Severus had Niger's wife and children put to death and the Niger estates confiscated.

But a secret offspring survived and was smuggled out. When he came of age he was told the tale of his parentage; the tale was handed on generation after generation, a festering sore that finally impelled Pedro to act.

Niger would have been a match for Severus, Pedro believed, if Albinus hadn't given his support. If Pedro could kill Albinus, then *everything* would change. His relative Pescennius Niger was beaten by the combined effort of Severus and Albinus. Ironic that in effect Niger was beaten by Albinus, Black by White.

Kyler whistled. "You risked winking out of existence so you could alter your family's past history?"

"I had the opportunity, I had to take it."

"Pedro Niger, you will not be able to attempt this again," Tertia said.

"Are you sure?" Kyler asked.

In response, Tertia pulled a bracelet from her satchel and swiftly snipped it on Niger's wrist. "This time-tag will summon a tribunal to your arrival site; they will be waiting for you, Pedro Niger. They will implant a subdermal time-tag in your body. Any attempt to use a Zygma projector will result in your instant annihilation."

Face crestfallen, Niger glared at Kyler and then Tertia.

"Here." She tossed the recall beacon amulet and Niger caught it. "Now, go."

Niger pressed the concealed button on the amulet. He then shimmered, vanishing from sight.

"Did you get his weapon?" Kyler asked.

"Yes, it's in the bag with the teeth, metal rod, Bulmer's ruined slimfone, and the shard of stone inscription."

Wolves howled again.

"Time to go," she said, clasping Kyler's hand. They both activated the recall buttons on their anklets.

XVI

As they returned to the London theater site, Kyler steadied himself. He was weak, hungry, bruised and battered. Tertia supported him on his wounded side.

"Welcome back," exclaimed Damon.

"Hi, Uncle D. You seem happy—your jaunt was a success?"

"Yep. Napoleon definitely wasn't murdered. And it stays that way. How about you?" Then he gazed admiringly at Tertia. "So, is this Tertia, your girlfriend?"

"Continuity girl," Kyler corrected. "Tertia's been a big help, since I didn't have you to hold my hand."

Damon studied Tertia with amused curiosity. "Continuity? As in the Flix?"

She nodded.

"I've never seen you around."

"I'm a hangover from the previous regime …"

"Well, honey, you're the kind of hangover I wouldn't mind having," Damon chuckled.

"Uncle D!"

Tertia grinned. "It's all right, Kyler. I can take a joke, and I appreciate word-play. Nothing is meant by it."

"Okay. Hey, Uncle, what can you tell me about a Zygma projector from the future? We met a guy from there—*our* future."

Damon shrugged. "Sennacherib can fill you in, I'm sure. It's all a bit too quantum-entangled for my liking." He saluted Tertia. "Nice meeting you, lass. Glad you brought my nephew back in one piece." He eyed Kyler's wounds. "Well, almost in one piece …"

* * *

At the first opportunity, Tertia and Kyler checked the chronovisor. There were a few minor architectural changes shimmering now, but no hint of ancient Roman structures. Kyler let loose a sigh of relief. "Mission successful," he said.

Then they went off to get health-checked. A robo-doc treated Kyler's wounds and then he went to get showered and to change clothes.

When they returned to give a briefing to Sennacherib, they both wore jeans, a T-shirt and sneakers; Tertia's T-shirt and jeans looked a lot better on her, Kyler reckoned.

After their debriefing, Sennacherib said, "Of course that druid you met, Ambrosius, he was the origin of the Merlin legend."

"The magician?" Kyler said.

"Yes. Not much is known about him. It's believed he was the son of a Roman consul, but rebelled against Rome and fled to southern Scotland."

"I thought he was based in Wales—or even Cornwall."

"He was. There might not have been a great deal of social mobility in those far-off days, but druids traveled the land all the time. That might explain the legends of Merlin's caves and seats throughout the kingdom."

"Visiting King Arthur's Camelot sounds appealing," Kyler mused.

"You'd be disappointed," Tertia said. "It's nothing like the Flix myth."

Kyler sighed. "It's tempting, sometimes, to alter history's course for the good, isn't it?"

"Don't follow Wilde's dictum, my friend," Tertia whispered.

"What's that?"

"The only way to get rid of temptation is to yield to it."

Winking at her, he said, "I'll remember that in future."

"Ah, the future," Sennacherib chipped in. "Your observations were correct, Kyler. The Zygma projector *does* come from the future, *your* future. How else could artefacts from there become focus objects to enable jaunts to the future?"

"I have the distinct feeling you only tell us so much, Sennacherib."

"Need to know basis. I'm programmed that way."

Tertia changed the subject. "I'll put Niger's weapon in the props room. Perhaps sometime it can be used as a focus object into the future."

"I'd like to see this props room of yours," Kyler said.

She shook her head. "Sorry, but I regret that it's out of bounds … to humans."

"Humans?" He stared at her. "What kind of answer is that?"

She smiled, wide, generous, almost loving. "Kyler, you mean you didn't guess?"

"Guess?" He released a laugh. "No way you're an alien."

"No, I'm not. Actually, I'm an android."

"Is this a joke? I saw you bleed."

Without a hint of embarrassment, she lifted her T-shirt and revealed her bare torso. There was no scar tissue.

Kyler hesitated, automatically reaching out, but refrained from touching her.

"Go on, palpate," she whispered.

Her skin was soft, velvety, and warm. Unblemished—and intact.

He glared at Sennacherib. "Does Uncle Damon know?"

"Yes. He worked with one of Tertia's companions in another time-stream. Before you joined the team."

Feeling an uncomfortable warm glow suffuse his cheeks, Kyler eyed Tertia and croaked, "There are *more* of you?"

Tertia nodded. "There are five other androids who have been dispersed throughout various timelines: Prima, Secunda, Quarta, Quinta, and Sexta. We were created at the same juncture as the Zygma projector. The intention was to only send us to fix time anomalies, but it soon became obvious that the human element was necessary. We androids don't get involved in all time jaunts, just certain difficult or intractable ones."

Kyler stared at Tertia. "That time-tag and your knowledge of the tribunal waiting for Niger ... You're from the future as well?" he croaked.

"Yes. We—along with Sennacherib and his predecessors—were designed by a brilliant Syrian refugee."

"Hence the names given to the AI systems?"

"Precisely," Sennacherib exclaimed.

"Wait till I see my uncle."

Both Tertia and Sennacherib laughed, a strange combination of sounds, and then Kyler joined in with them.

Taking hold of Tertia's hand, Kyler said, "Join me for a drink?"

"I'd like that," she said. "But first you'd better see this—it's a letter that your uncle gave me while you changed. He reckoned it might be of interest." She dug it out the back pocket of her jeans and handed it over. "Postmarked Bistritz, 4 May 1897."

†

We Fell Below the Earth

1

Chief Inspector Caine Irving of Scotland Yard (Paranormal Investigations Agency) leaned on his ornate hawthorn walking stick and scratched his bald head with his free hand. He eyed the naked female cadaver on the morgue's scanner table, her head near the huge orifice. She'd probably been a fine-looking woman; in her twenties, he guessed; long blonde hair, a firm chin, with staring gray eyes that appeared startled at the realization that their owner had entered the afterlife prematurely.

The first time he'd seen a wide-eyed subject prepared for an autopsy scan, he'd queried why the eyes hadn't been closed. He'd been told that the scanalysis sometimes detected tell-tale light impressions on the retina from the final instant of life that might be deciphered later.

This latest victim's complexion was exceedingly pale and her flesh appeared deflated, doubtless due to the manner of her death. Apart from severe bruising at the throat, there were no obvious indications of violence. The plastic toe-tag didn't show a name, only a file number and date of delivery. Thankfully for the sake of his queasy stomach, the autopsy butchering was no longer necessary on the nameless nude. The table she lay on was part of the virtuautopsy machine, a combined 3D MRI and CT scanner. Next to the table was an array of heart-lung monitors, which would insert contrast solutions into the corpse's circulation; the robot links were presently pumping those solutions into the body now. Once the scans were complete, the pathologists would have a virtual form of the body that could be referred to repeatedly and analyzed. "So, Charlie, this is yet another one?"

"Definitely, Caine." Dr. Charlotte Thornley gazed at the corpse, her bronze eyes blazing into his. Often, she'd raged at the waste of human life she witnessed. Her job meant she saw more than most. "The same as the last four," she said resignedly. "Just like the others, the blood loss is enormous." Which explained the deflation. "I only hope the collapse of the veins and arteries won't impede the insertion of the contrast fluids."

"The others were okay, weren't they?"

"Yes, most of them, anyway. We had some blockages and a couple of solution leaks, but Hodge dealt with them." She gestured at her assistant who hovered over another corpse, preparing it for her attention later. "So, we were still able to obtain satisfactory data."

"Any early conclusions?"

"Well," she said, grimacing, "we know there was no sign of blood spatter at the discovery scene."

All five corpses had been found outside the London dome. Despite that, his bailiwick encompassed the entirety of London, in-dome and out-dome. "Yet you're convinced that this murder wasn't committed somewhere else and the body moved?"

"We've been over this." A touch of irritability in her tone. "I've viewed the scene vids. Every indication suggests the woman died where she was found." She leant forward, pointing to the neck of the deceased. "See, identical marks?"

"Yup." There were two small punctures in the skin, with indentations between and around them. He held up a hand. "I know, definitely not a snake-bite."

"All four earlier victims indicate that the blood was sucked from holes like these. And not by using a couple of syringes; the incisions are ragged, definitely made by teeth since we've measured the other indentations. She suffered trauma to the puncture site only. Again, it's the carotid artery rather than the jugular vein that's been penetrated."

"So, nothing new so far." Irving let out a sigh. "The killer is consistent and knows human anatomy."

Charlie bobbed her head in agreement. "He—or she—prefers the oxygenated blood carried by the carotid rather than deoxygenated from the jugular."

"Sort of favors good over bad blood?"

"In a manner of speaking. Naturally, oxygenated blood is more beneficial; the stuff of life, if you will.

73

I'll start the machine and get busy on the post mortem. When I get back to you, I suspect the verdict will be the same as the others."

"Vampire?"

She glared at him. "The first, it could have been a hoax. The second, a coincidence. Now, with this fifth victim, I'd say you've got one thirsty blood-sucker to contend with."

He tapped his stick on the floor. "So, vampire or not?"

"I deal in facts, Caine. Not the sensational or the supernatural. That's your department."

"We've closed down all the illegal clinics that siphon off blood from fresh corpses to sell to the war effort. What's left? Vampires. Stands to reason."

"Reason? I'll reserve judgement for now."

"Okay, Miss Skeptic."

Caine fished in his jacket and held up an envelope. "This was found in our corpse's skirt pocket. It may be a clue."

"It's bulky." She glanced at the address. "Continuity Inc.?"

2

Damon Cole led Chief Inspector Irving into the CI office. The plain-clothes policeman was in his early fifties; imposing, broad-shouldered, six feet six inches tall, with a barrel chest. "It's a while since we met, Chief Inspector."

Irving nodded, piercing gray eyes shining. "The Absent Scientist."

"That's it. Absent in more ways than one, wasn't he?"

"You helped me crack the case." He lightly tapped the wooden stick against his leg. "Though it left its mark. I must admit, it took me a while to accept the truth about your Zygma machine's capabilities, remember?"

"I do. And now you're a convert. So, what can CI do for you?"

"I appreciate you giving me the time, Mr. Cole. We're investigating a number of similar murders that imply a serial killer is at large."

"Here, in the dome?"

Irving shook his head. "Not as far as we can determine. All of the dead have been found outside the dome. Which makes our job that much harder. Deptford, Tower Hamlets cemetery, and Hackney."

"Both sides of the river."

"Yes. But, even so, fairly localized."

"Tower Hamlets, that's not far from Whitechapel."

"The deaths have no similarity to the Ripper, Mr. Cole."

"Glad to hear it." Damon stroked his chin, fingers rasping on bristles. "Though it would be interesting to go to Whitechapel, to that time, and perhaps solve the riddle, don't you think?"

"From an academic and professional viewpoint, yes. But that's all."

Damon held up his hand. "I agree. Even if we could identify the Ripper, we couldn't announce it before our present time."

"Tempting, though, Mr. Cole, very tempting."

"Are there any clues? After five deaths, I'd suspect you'd have some lead."

Irving sighed. "No. All of the bodies have lost an excessive amount of blood, but never any blood-spatter at the scene. All the evidence confirms the victims died where they were found. In fact, the only clue we have to date is this envelope found on the latest dead woman." The inspector held it out for Damon to view.

"It's addressed to our company."

Irving handed it over.

Damon looked askance. "You haven't opened it?"

"No. I thought I'd let you do that."

As he slid his finger through the back flap of the envelope, slitting it open, Damon remarked, "Seems odd, handling an actual letter. I can't remember the last time I did this." He slid out another smaller envelope; this one had already been slit open and it was aged, its date of posting: the 5th of May, 1897. The postmark: Bistritz. "It's addressed to a Miss Mina Sheridan." He looked at the inspector. "Do you know the name?"

"Never heard of her, but that isn't surprising, is it?"

"No, of course." Why would the inspector know a Mina Sheridan from the 1890s? With care now, Damon removed the contents of this second envelope and read the three handwritten sheets.

Bistritz,
4 May, 1897

Dearest Mina,

My profoundest apologies for not committing myself to paper to you before this day but the long and arduous journey has been decidedly hectic, more of which anon, and it has taken me all my time to maintain my journal in short-hand.

I hope this missive finds you well. As I write I am ensconced in a cubicle constructed of ancient black oak, near to a crackling fire at one end of this old hostelry, The Golden Krone Hotel. But a moment ago I looked up, to perceive the embers of a ravaged log, and I could have sworn therein was an image of your dear friend Lucy. Whimsical, I know! I must strongly resist a tendency towards journalism when writing to my family, friends and loved ones!

Since leaving hearth and home I have had no communication from my prospective host, but I have managed to follow his travel instructions to the letter. It has been quite an adventure!

The journey began in earnest when I embarked upon the packet steamer 'Dark Star' bound for Dubrovnik. The cabin appointments left a great deal to be desired, with coal-dust from the boiler-room seeming to cover everything.

That first evening, after an atrocious greasy meal, I had settled myself to write to you, but alas there blew up out of nowhere one of the fiercest storms ever encountered by our bluff but likeable captain Conrad. Much to my shame, I retired to my uncompromisingly hard bunk where, feeling awfully sorry for myself, I lay for the entire crossing.

As you know, I have crossed the Atlantic to my cousins in New York on several occasions, and visited Uncle Silas in Eire, but I have never succumbed to 'mal de mer' before.

You can be assured that it is not a pleasant experience! It is not simply an out-of-sorts sensation in one's stomach: one's head swims, as if it too is adrift in the very storm that belabours the vessel, and there is a disorienting muzziness engulfing the brain so that any cohesive thought is tantamount to being impossible to accomplish. A weariness encompasses the limbs, and a shivering weakness pervades the very soul. Sacrilegious to remark, but at one's lowest ebb one almost wishes for the Great Adventure, death, itself!

Happily, on our approach to the port, the sea calmed and these varied ailments deserted me, though I confess to being left like a piece of damp cloth, wrung through.

The carriage my host promised to provide was indeed awaiting me at the quayside. It was a splendid affair, most resembling a landau, with four strong black horses, all caparisoned in shining leather and brass livery.

A rather cadaverous pair of men perched on its high seat, fancifully reminding me of those crows we used to stone in farmer Bayliss' field! My host's two retainers were taciturn to the point of rudeness, yet they speedily processed me through the official formalities and, once my baggage was installed in the luggage compartment, we were on our way.

If you believe our coaches are unpleasant contrivances, with the ubiquitous dust and bone-jarring springs, do not ever consider journeying in these continental contraptions! Within the hour I seemed to be bruised all over.

At the outset, the plush upholstery had smelled of luxurious leather, but in no time at all the interior was clogged with a russet-colored dust.

I shall complete this epistle to you later. I am assured there is a post office at our next place of call for we must journey on this very night before the storm breaks.

Your loving Jonathan.

Carpathians,
5 May, 1897

Dearest Mina,

Disaster struck! Last night, while our coachman drove our poor beasts pell-mell through a violent rainstorm, a wheel sheered from the vehicle. He was catapulted off the mountainside to an awful certain death, while I myself barely escaped with a bruised jaw and a sprained ankle.

Fortunately, the surviving retainer, Arpad, knows the mountains well. He called some mediaeval curse upon the driver who had lost his life for his impetuousness, then directed me to follow him up through a winding overgrown defile. Rainwater sluiced down the rocks from above, and I was very soon drenched. I abandoned my portmanteau but struggled manfully with the carpetbag. Arpad deigned not to assist me.

Eventually, Arpad found this shelter. It is an old ruined fortress, the walls long ago dismantled to supply the local populace with dry-stone walls and low-ceilinged hovels.

The rain has ceased. I must confess to an uneasiness in the presence of Arpad. He is a great hulking fellow, with a low brow, beady black eyes and enormous hands. He hardly ever speaks, and when he does it is in guttural fractured Romanian.

But as I gaze out the slit window, across these mountains, irrational worry departs.

If only you could share this view with me, dearest Mina!

The condensation from the night's rain has now become a romantic mist, half-clouding the mauve and gray peaks, with the rays of the rising sun glinting on outcrops of unblemished snow and twinkling ice. And the air is so fresh. This land must surely be blessed!

I broke off writing for a moment as Arpad explained we must be getting on. He even gave me two swigs of his slivovitz, a rather tart plum brandy, which perked me up considerably.

I hope to write again soon, my dear. But I must close and slip this letter into its envelope. According to

Arpad, his master will endeavour to send this on to you from his ancestral demesne.

Strangely, I feel a trifle light-headed, probably on account of that liquor - a little sleepy. I am sure that Arpad will look after me, as his master has expressed a great interest in my writing style.

Yes, indeed, I am greatly looking forward to meeting Count Erdel in his Transylvanian castle.

Yours, forever, Jonathan.

* * *

"The dead woman can't be the recipient, Mina, obviously," Damon said. "You know, the name Mina rings a vague bell." He glanced up as Tertia entered wearing a T-shirt, jeans and sneakers.

Damon made hasty introductions then gave Tertia the three sheets. "What do you make of these?"

She rapidly scanned the pages.

"Have you heard of a woman called Mina?" Damon asked her.

She inclined her head, blinked. "Most odd. The names Mina and Jonathan relate to Bram Stoker's classic horror novel *Dracula*. Mina Murray was the fiancée of Jonathan Harker, a solicitor visiting Count Dracula in Transylvania."

Inspector Irving's complexion paled and his eyes squinted, surveying her. "Vampires … from 300-year-old literature … You have remarkable recall, young lady."

"Thank you, Inspector. It's actually 326 years since that book was published." Damon noted that she didn't bother to explain that her storage system held a vast library of information concerning fiction and history.

Damon slapped his forehead with the heel of his hand. "That's it, of course! Thanks, Tertia." He tapped the sheets of paper. "But the names are different—she's Mina Sheridan. And the count referred to here isn't Dracula but Erdel."

"Perhaps the letters are genuine," Tertia suggested, "and they came into Stoker's possession. Then he used them as a source for his novel."

Irving cleared his throat. "I don't like this at all." He tapped his stick on the floor. "The parallels are uncanny."

Damon chuckled. "Well, that's what you deal in, isn't it, Inspector? The uncanny."

"That's the truth. I've posited to our pathologist that vampirism is responsible. After all, our murder victims have been drained of several pints of blood ..."

"Vampires?" Damon whistled and then grinned. "No, they're pure myth. Everyone knows that."

Tertia lanced him with a cautionary look. "Certain evidence suggests there may be some truth in the myth," she said. "They may be more than figments of imagination, suitable for novels, Flix and poetry. I recall a twentieth-century, young poet's words, just a fragment, *We Fell Below the Earth*: 'Drain the life from the corpse again, And let us to leave, Let us live ...' Something like that, anyway."

"Yes, but that's imagination, not fact," Damon said.

"My blood-drained corpses are fact, Mr. Cole."

"I'll access the databank," Tertia said. "We may have a record of a time-jump to 1897."

"How will that help?" Irving asked.

"I know it's unlikely, but if there were vampires around then," Tertia explained, "they must have died out or been killed off since we haven't had any evidence of their existence in modern history."

"Or they've gone underground and never troubled mankind until now?" Damon suggested.

"That's an unwelcome possibility," she conceded. "Alternatively, the vampire's appearance in our time is sudden and very recent."

"You're wondering if there is a vampire here now then the Zygma projector must have been used to bring it here?"

"Not necessarily," she countered. "If they exist, the undead can survive for hundreds of years—unless discovered and disposed of in some ritualistic manner."

"But why are we troubled now?" Irving queried, fiddling with his walking stick. "None of my previous cases have involved anything remotely related to vampirism."

"That is troubling," Tertia said. "I still think we should check the records, to be sure." She put the sheets in the envelope. "Can I show these to Kyler?"

Damon nodded. "I'd like his input."

Tertia turned on her heel and made for the door. "I'll get back to you soon, Damon, Inspector."

3

His wounds from his last jaunt still smarting, even after the Robodoc had efficiently dealt with them, Kyler lowered the handwritten sheets to the desk and eased himself back in his chair, studying Tertia.

She sat at a desk opposite his, her feet up, fingers steepled against her pursed lips. Deep in thought, he reckoned. Or, rather, her electronic brain was sifting through a mass of data. He almost fancied he could hear the artificial synapses firing off.

"A little more of that poetry seems apt, Kyler."

"Really?"

"It's from another fragment—*Writing Letters Alone in the Light of the Alcove*—'Time Travel, And Visions, Magic in the dampened veld of African myth, And other graceless, But ever-charming vexations, Endless to our cheering phantasmagoric imaginations.'"

"I go along with the time travel, and visions, obviously, though I'm not sure about the African veld."

"Yes, but isn't it strangely sublime?"

"I'm not one for poetry, Tertia. Sorry. Hey, while you search your memory banks, I'll do a more mundane 'find'—time-jumps to the 1800s." He rapidly fingered keys, feeling quite adept now. A haze of dropdown windows appeared and he discarded some, retained others and drilled down for more information. Finally, he hit interesting and relevant data. Historian Tom Matheson had written to Time Corps, seeking approval for his research into vampirism in the Carpathians in the late 1800s. Kyler quickly scanned through

Matheson's written request, and the authority's final response, which was negative. At least he had the historian's address: it was on the request form.

Now he had a name and an address.

"Your grin tells me you've got a lead," Tertia said, standing behind him.

He started slightly, surprised that she could leave her desk and get so close without him noticing. "Don't creep up on me like that."

"I don't creep," she said, grinning. "I might perambulate in silent mode, however."

"Well, switch off that function and walk like a human woman."

"Very well." She blinked rapidly for two seconds, and jiggled her hips provocatively. "Rectified. Now, what have you found?"

With an effort he ignored her hipshot stance and showed her, adding, "I can't find anything in the Time Corps records for Matheson taking a time-jump to 1897 or any period prior to 1820. There's no record of anyone else utilizing Bulmer's duplicate Zygma projector, so Matheson might also have his own machine, which is what their hidden records suggests." He eyed Tertia. "Time you used your surge probe."

Tertia delved into her capacious shoulder bag and produced the flat-screen tablet, hastily flicked in data and within half a minute, the screen blipped at her.

"Definitely déjà vu," Kyler said, laughing. "That's his address. We need to go there and locate Tom Matheson."

"Before we do that, let's check with your uncle."

"I don't need his permission, you know. I'm a field agent, just like him."

"He needs to know your lead so he won't waste time covering the same ground."

"Oh, yes, of course." They left for Damon's office.

A few minutes later, after Chief Inspector Irving had been introduced, Damon Cole said, "Good work, Kyler." He gestured at the policeman. "I think the inspector and I should investigate Matheson's home, while you and Tertia trace Tom Matheson's steps in Transylvania in1897."

"But I made the link, found the address," Kyler remonstrated.

"I know." Damon held up a hand. "But you're younger than me." He stretched, hands massaging his lower back. "Those time jumps are beginning to take it out of me. Go with Tertia, investigate, and return as soon as you can."

"The action's here, Uncle D, not in 1897."

"Knowing you, Kyler, the action's wherever you're at."

* * *

Special dispensation had been given to Kyler so that the "props room," situated next door to the theater, was no longer out of bounds to him. This was his first visit. He found the enormous repository chamber was more like a warehouse. He was excited to see the variety, colors and breadth of period costumes and assorted items from the past.

Now, he wore a gray flannel jacket; it was tight-fitting with short sleeves, a waistcoat and light gray trousers. His white shirt, with tight collar and a bow-tie was accompanied by a brown derby set on a slant, neatly complementing his apparel. Tertia wore a deep blue and white striped blouse with puffed sleeves, and an ankle-length dark pleated skirt.

Whatever the time period he planned to visit, he always felt more comfortable carrying a weapon of some kind. Not all field agents felt the same, he learned. One or two preferred to rely on their wits alone. Good luck to them. He knew for a fact that he'd only escaped from a number of tight spots by wielding a weapon. For this jaunt, he chose a Remington Model 1875 revolver and the 1892 Winchester lever-action repeating rifle. "Neat, huh?" he told Tertia. "They both use .44-40 ammunition, so that'll make it easier. What are you taking?"

"I thought it more appropriate to select a British firearm from the period, since the correspondent Jonathan seems English." She held up a .45 revolver. "This Webley Mk III will do. And a laser, of course." The latest laser weapon was designed in the form of a fob-watch; depressing the winder activated it.

The focus object was the letter from Transylvania. "Let's hope that it's genuine," Kyler remarked.

"I verified the age of the paper before I brought the sheets to you," Tertia told him.

"That's a relief, then."

Tertia took his hand; her touch was warm, reassuring. "Let's go." She led him out the big door, voice-locked it, and they made their way through an underground linked corridor into the theater; all the time he held her hand, pleased to feel her warmth and connection. If only she were human.

Passing a number of theatrical flats, they came to the set for a horror melodrama popular some years ago on the Net.

All the wood furniture was clunky and aged. It appeared to be the vestibule of a hotel.

Damon wheeled in the Zygma projector. "Ready, guys? Got your recall beacons?"

"Yes," Kyler said, holding up a 3D-printed snuff-box. Tertia held up a reticule, then stuffed it in her leather shoulder bag. "We're set to go." Kyler's gut clenched, the usual reflex anticipation he experienced. A slight squeeze of Tertia's hand in his was soothing.

The projector's quartz eye began spinning. Lights flickered and dimmed as the machine drained the energy from the entire block of buildings. Some would suffer a brief power surge. The fission pile in the basement activated, and the quartz eye spun faster, and pallid radiation soaked Kyler and Tertia.

Zygma particles unpicked the surrounding reality, instantaneously wrenching them from London's West End, flinging them through the chronosphere, thrusting them into nineteenth century Transylvania.

4

Voice-operated, the gull-wing doors raised on the gray Mercedes XXL-22; the hydraulics emitted a faint susurration. Inspector Irving slid behind the driver's console, stowing his walking stick in a specially adapted sleeve in the ceiling. Damon sat in the passenger seat. The doors hissed again and closed. Their seat-belts automatically embraced them.

"Destination?" the chip-voice requested.

Inspector Irving gave Tom Matheson's Blackheath address.

"That is outside the dome," the car responded.

"I know. Take appropriate precautions." Irving turned his attention to a file that appeared on the console screen; slowly, he finger flicked through the electronic pages. Kyler noticed it was a comprehensive biography of Matheson.

The electric motor engaged and the Mercedes smoothly left the curb. "Anti-personnel cloak engaged." The early driverless cars had been prey to hijack gangs; the hijackers would step in front of the vehicle and it would auto-stop, becoming immobile, allowing the gang members enough time to smash the windscreen, threaten and rob the occupants. Now, the Mercedes would stop if an obstruction presented itself, but the impervious electromagnetic shield would prevent any incursion by the ill-disposed.

Driverless, the vehicle glided through the pristine streets of the city, avoiding any hint of traffic congestion, anticipating delays and red lights, appropriately coordinating its movement to blend in with the flow of other transport, lane-switching for maximum efficiency.

"Matheson is a popular historian," Irving remarked. "I recall seeing a Docuflic last year. He was studying lycanthropy."

"Werewolves." Damon shook his head. "And now vampires. Have we shunted into a fantasy parallel universe?"

Irving chuckled, jabbing a finger at the image of Matheson on the screen. "According to this file, he believes the discovery of time travel—even though it's regulated and you strive to protect history—heralded in a sequence of parallel time-streams. Where before these time-streams were 'what if' scenarios, now they've split into different realities. In some, fiction is fact."

"I'm sure the theory sells his books." Damon studied the image on the console screen. Matheson possessed a frantic head of fair hair, bifocals over green-gray eyes, and a nose that would be at home gracing an ancient Roman senator. "I can't subscribe to his theory, though. Otherwise, we at CI would be wasting our efforts, wouldn't we? Which time-stream history would we be safeguarding?"

"A valid point, Mr. Cole."

"Western exit in one minute," the vehicle informed them. At the dome's signposted exit gate an electronic eye interrogated the vehicle's windscreen identification glyphs: authorized police vehicle. Then the gate slid up, the opening's width providing barely sufficient room for their passage. No sooner had they driven through than the gate rapidly shut. Damon checked the rear-view screen; he knew that if any pedestrian had attempted to exit on the tail of the car, they'd have been zapped into unconsciousness. Out-domers had appropriate channels to negotiate before they were allowed access.

As soon as they exited the dome, the contrast was marked. Through the rear view screen Damon could see the dome, Plexiglas tarnished with grime, emissions from munitions factories, and white flakes from the crematoria. Cleaning only occurred every two months: insane sanitation rules.

Ahead of them loomed dilapidated office blocks and derelict dwellings. Rows of filthy houses sped past on either side, many of them abandoned and boarded up, the majority daubed with graffiti and anti-war slogans.

He knew that London was no different from any other major British city, each of them protected by domes. Outside the bubbles could be found the engine-houses for the country, supplying the factories, weapon shops, equipment and technology needed to sustain the status quo. In tandem with the industries, the countryside was a vast patchwork complex of polythene-garbed fields, force-growing vegetables and fruit. Most of the populace by default was vegetarian now; only certain enclaves bred animals for slaughter, their meat bartered at exorbitant prices. Underground lived, appropriately, the underclass; whenever factories required additional manpower, recruitment-gangs were sent to acquire them from the underground and press them into work. Damon glimpsed flocks of birds soaring above the rooftops, a delightful sight now alien to the denizens within the dome.

After an hour, the Mercedes braked gently outside a block of apartments in Blackheath. "You have arrived at your destination," the car informed them.

At one time—perhaps ten years ago, Damon reckoned—the area would have been attractive, but now it was rundown, weeds poking through the pedestrian pathways, burst plastic bags of garbage littering the gutters, scavenging children sifting through wheeled bins, cars jacked up on bricks, and over against a wall huddled two homeless people sharing a thin blanket. Street lighting was inferior to that found in the dome; it seemed that many lights were broken, anyway. Night was descending, he noticed. A gradual process, unlike that experienced in the dome. A flickering porch light beckoned at the apartment block entrance; that flickering could be due to a power surge from a projector, Damon surmised.

"Anti-personnel protection nullified. Take care." The gull-wings opened, their hissing sound almost drowned by the passing tuk-tuks and motor-scooters, the only affordable transport for the poor and the dome-excluded.

Irving retrieved his stick and he and Damon stepped out; the car doors shut promptly. Irving said, "Invoke anti-personnel protection."

The car responded to his voice: its lights flickered orange for an instant, and then it murmured: "Awaiting your return. Have a nice stay."

* * *

Black night pressed against the skylight windows of the morgue. Sitting at her desk, Dr. Charlotte Thornley briefly thought about her assistant, Nevil Hodge. He'd clocked off, more or less on time. She couldn't blame him. He probably had a life. She really wanted to get home to a hot shower and a glass of chilled white wine, but first she decided to scan the computer files. Curiosity, she admitted, was one of her many besetting sins.

This so-called "blood-drain case" annoyed her. She was disappointed to note that the previous four murder victims were still unnamed. Surely Caine and his people could have identified some of the dead? Were they getting lax? Of course, since all four murder victims had been found outside the dome; that had hindered enquiries: out-domers resented in-domers, which was understandable. Since the bodies were unidentified, she wasn't surprised to see that they were unclaimed. Yet again, she wondered if they'd missed any clues on the corpses. She pulled up the virtuautopsy analysis on her desktop screen, but it was no help. Like her predecessor, she preferred contact with the actual dead, the morbid flesh. She left her desk and made her way to the refrigerated room.

Donning a thermal jacket from the peg alongside the door, she tapped the keypad and the door's seal hissed; she entered.

Her breath streamed in front of her, wispy. There were three tiers of metal drawers on either side of the long room, each labelled. Several showed "MT"— which meant empty. Only suspicious deaths resided here, so it was absurdly comforting that there were not too many of those.

Charlie slid open the drawer of the first blood-drained victim.

She let out a gasp. The drawer was empty.

Damn Hodge, he must have released the body but not updated the system. She slammed the drawer shut. The sound echoed in the room. *I'll have words with him tomorrow*, she thought. She yanked open the second victim's drawer. No corpse inside. Hurriedly, she checked the other two—all four were missing.

What the hell? No way had Hodge omitted to update the system for all four.

She gave a start as she thought she heard a faint sound, a kind of scraping noise. Definitely nearby. Hodge had left over an hour ago. She knew she was the only person on the premises; nobody else—living, that is—was in this room. "At least victim number five must still be here," she told herself, her voice echoing as she opened the next drawer.

And the body *was* there.

She let out an involuntary laugh.

But then her laughter choked on her indrawn breath.

The corpse slowly sat up, the white sheet falling away, its eyes dark and staring. The dead woman's skin glowed translucently under the ceiling's LED lighting.

Charlie swore and backed off.

The naked undead woman seemed unsure of her surroundings. Thin bony hands grasping the edge of the drawer, she—it?—clambered out in ungainly fashion and stumbled as its feet touched the floor.

Then it raised its head, the eyes sunken, dark with red rims, and stared at Charlie.

It sniffed the air, opened its mouth and grinned, revealing teeth, the two lateral incisors larger and more pointed than the others around them.

Its ungainly stride faltering, as if unaccustomed to the use of its limbs, the undead woman stepped towards Charlie.

Hastily backing to the door, Charlie opened it. She dashed through and slammed it shut before the undead woman could reach her.

The refrigeration seal hissed. Charlie's finger jabbed the keypad, locked the door, and then she sank down to the floor with her back against the wall. "Caine," she said, on the verge of hysteria, "I'm definitely a convert now!"

5

Kyler and Tertia stood in the large courtyard of a castle. A multitude of stars glimmered in the night sky. Torches burned in metal brackets on the ancient walls. "We made it?" Kyler whispered, eyes scanning the empty colonnades.

"The absence of electric light suggests we're in the right time." Tertia nodded at the huge studded wooden door in the entrance portico. "Pull the bell, perhaps?"

Stepping forward, Kyler tugged at the metal ring. Distantly, a bell rang. "Either the bell's very big and loud or the walls and door are thin."

"The former, I reckon."

Abruptly, metal bolts rattled and the door creaked. A large pudgy hand appeared around the edge of the door, followed by a lined face mostly in shadow. "You rang?" the man grated, his beady black eyes glinting beneath a low brow.

"We're travelers," Kyler improvised, doffing his derby hat. "Our coach has lost a wheel. We wonder if you could accommodate us tonight."

"That is most unfortunate, dear sir," the man said. "I regret that the master is away at present …"

"Arpad, don't leave our visitors on the doorstep," a woman's voice commanded. "Bring them in."

Bowing ingratiatingly, the man called Arpad whispered, "My apologies, please do enter." He took Kyler's hat and beckoned with a flourish of his big hand; he stepped aside, a man of large stature though slightly bent forward.

As they passed the great hulking man, Kyler exchanged a knowing look with Tertia. She'd noticed too. Arpad was referred to in Jonathan's letter some three hundred years ago. It could be a common name for the region, of course, or a family moniker handed down.

"You are most kind," Tertia said as Arpad shut and bolted the door.

They were in a large vestibule. Wall-sconces flickered with torch-light; directly ahead was a staircase that led to a second-floor landing with a balcony. For an instant, Kyler thought he saw movement in the shadows up there; then it was gone.

Loping ahead of them, Arpad said, "This way, please." He led them across the echoing tiled floor towards a tall doorway on their right; two other sets of doors on the left of the staircase were closed. A faint ruddy glow issued from the doorway.

"Lady Lilith," Arpad said, bowing at the door, "the two visitors."

Kyler let Tertia enter first. "Ever the gentleman," Tertia whispered.

"No," he responded in a husky voice, "I know you can absorb more information than me, and faster too."

"The age of chivalry is dead," she riposted.

"Welcome," exclaimed the slender woman standing at the hearth, where a log fire sent up red and yellow flames. The fire and the wall-torches conspired to lend the room a warm red glow, a color that predominated, as the woman wore a flowing red gown, held a glass of red wine, and had long flowing red tresses. Her garment was slit up the center to reveal a gold lace full-length carmine shift. "I am Lady Lilith Erdel. And who might I be addressing?"

Kyler bowed slightly and gestured at Tertia. "I'm Kyler Knightly, and this is Tertia—"

"Tertia Knightly, Kyler Knightly, you are both welcome," Lady Lilith interjected. "I am impressed, you understand my country's language so well."

He wondered if Tertia had another name. She'd said before that "Tertia will suffice." It seemed that people assumed they were a couple. For a fleeting moment, he relished that thought, and then reminded himself that she was an android. "We were adept students," he replied.

"Commendable. Please, take some wine with me." Lady Lilith pointed to the drinks on the sideboard on the left of the door. "I'm afraid we only stock red," she added. "I am sure it will appeal to your palates."

Arpad hastened there and filled two crystal glasses with red wine from a carafe. The rich liquid glimmered in the firelight as the servant carried the tray to them.

Tertia took her glass and sniffed the bouquet. She nodded faintly to Kyler, indicating that her olfactory senses had not detected anything other than wine. He took his glass and raised it to Lady Lilith. "Noroc!" he said, in toasting her health.

Clinking their glasses, Lilith replied, "Let us live long."

Kyler eyed Tertia and wondered about that.

He found the wine full-bodied, fruity and smooth; a pleasant after-taste lingered on the palate. Most unlike the artificial crap from his own time. He studied the rest of the room. The walls were decorated with shields bearing a variety of coats-of-arms, and swords and even a couple of crossbows. In one corner was a medieval suit of armor. Antique satin-covered chairs were placed randomly along the walls. "Nice place you have here," he said.

"It has been in our family for countless generations." Lilith sipped her wine and her thin lips shone wetly. She frowned. "You have no luggage?"

"We left it on the coach," he improvised.

Tertia added, "The driver will watch over it."

Lilith proffered her hand to Tertia. "Let Arpad relieve you of your bag, my dear."

Clutching the shoulder satchel to her, Tertia smiled. "No, I would rather hold onto it, if you don't mind."

"It is of no consequence." She swallowed the rest of the wine. "Arpad, show our visitors to the guest wing, please."

"It is most kind of you," Kyler said, hastily drinking his wine.

"Later, I will send Arpad to bring you down for the evening repast. You must be famished."

"Thank you again," Tertia said.

Arpad gestured at the door. "Follow me."

* * *

The darkness of night pervaded Nevil Hodge's soul. Deep within, he felt lost. Corrupted and now a mere puppet. As his driverless vehicle drove him—and his entourage—to his apartment, he wondered how he had succumbed.

It had been time for him to leave work; Dr. Thornley was still busy in the virtuautopsy room. Yet, foolishly, he'd responded to a scratching sound in one of the cadaver drawers. His heart had skipped, for sure. He'd thought he was hallucinating, but even when he stood up from his desk and paced the room for many minutes, the insistent noise didn't go away. He should have contacted Dr. Thornley; but she was busy elsewhere in the morgue. In fact, she'd probably have dismissed his concerns, and might even have considered dismissing him from his post.

He remembered opening the drawer. The corpse beneath the sheet was still, and silent. To be expected. It was his imagination, after all. Yet an unexpected impulse urged him to peel back the sheet, just to make sure.

The woman, the first victim in the blood-drain case, was unchanged. Her eyes were shut, normal procedure following the virtuautopsy scan. Such a pretty face—despite the lack of color. As he was about to cover the face again, the dead woman's eyes opened.

Colorless dark eyes.

Penetrating.

Mesmerizing.

His hands went limp. He lost all volition.

It was as though he viewed himself from afar, watching as he helped the dead woman out of her narrow confinement. Aware of her nakedness, he yanked the sheet from the drawer and draped it around her. She smiled; a "thank you," he supposed, and felt pleased about that recognition of his good manners.

Then, as if in a dream, he went from drawer to drawer, and released the other three women, draping them in white sheets too.

For a fleeting instant, vague rationality impinged and he fancied he was with a coven of ghosts.

Then, one after the other supped from his neck artery. He experienced an immense emotional high as they drank his blood. Absently, he noticed that they were careful not to splash too much; only the sheets were stained, ever so slightly, red.

No words passed any of their engorged lips, yet he "heard" their instructions.

He clocked off, the four sheet-draped ghosts in train, their toe-tags clacking as they walked.

He reflected that it must have been quite a sight as they all trooped across the parking lot to his vehicle. Though at this time of the evening there'd be nobody about to witness it; besides, the night-lighting was limited to conserve energy. It was a tight fit; some of the women giggled, a grating, rasping sound.

Now, ensconced in his apartment, he lay back on his bed and reveled in the attention of four naked women. Within a short while he was too weak to raise himself on an elbow. He watched and listened.

They spoke in clipped sentences. Sometimes, he wondered if they spoke at all; perhaps he heard their thoughts?

They made their plans. It included him only so far as supplying them with blood; sustenance, they termed it. He knew them only by the number of victimhood.

"Until the master comes for us," said One.

"He will not abandon us," intoned Two.

"Delicious though he is," said Three, licking her bloody lips, "this man is not enough to sustain all of us while we wait."

"I agree," said Four.

"We must obtain fresh blood," drooled One.

"Yes," exclaimed Four, "and in so doing, increase our brood."

6

"This place gives me the creeps," Kyler said in Anglic, pacing across the large somber bedroom to the high window. "And as for that Arpad, he's like something out of an old Flix soap." He peered through the thick glass. Below was the courtyard where they'd materialized.

"We need to speak with care, Kyler," Tertia whispered. "The walls may have ears."

He turned to face her. "But they won't know Anglic, will they?"

"It is not that far removed from English." She leaned close to him, touched his head. "I'll switch our linguachip to speak and translate in Continuity cypher."

She applied precise pressure and Kyler was surprised that he felt nothing. "Has it worked?"

"Yes. We must remember to switch it back before we next meet Lady Lilith or her staff."

"Staff? We've seen nobody else but Arpad." He moved to the huge four-poster bed and sat. It was firm, comfortable. Tonight, they'd have to sleep together to keep up appearances. Besides, he didn't relish being left alone in this creepy place. "What do we do now?"

She sat next to him, not touching. "We must locate Tom Matheson. He has to be here."

"What makes you so sure? If he's using his own machine, he could have returned to London by now."

"In which case," she said, lips curving, blue-gray eyes delving into his, "your uncle and the chief inspector will be there to meet him."

He stood awkwardly, pointing at the leather satchel on a straight-backed chair. "Did you bring that speckled ball thing? Can't you use that?"

"Ah, the Zygma particle detector …" She stood, retrieved the bag.

"That's it. Well, if he's in the castle that will pinpoint him, surely?"

"Indeed." She delved into the capacious satchel and pulled out the now familiar speckled ball. Three speckles glowed until Tertia tinkered, canceling their own markers, leaving only a single one glowing faint yellow.

"We'll have to sneak around the castle, I suppose, until it glows green?"

"That's one way." She smiled. "There is another, however."

She pulled out her slimfone, tapped a handful of icons and a blueprint of the castle appeared on the screen.

"Where'd you get that?"

"I put in an immediate request to Historical Plans as soon as I read those letters. The blueprint was delivered to my slimfone before we jumped here."

She tapped at the flat screen and held it up to face the wall. The screen glowed and then projected a magnified image of the blueprint on the wall. "Here, take this." She gave him the ball. "Slowly roll the particle detector over that image until we identify Matheson's whereabouts."

Kyler moved to the wall and complied.

Finally, the speckle glowed green.

103

Tertia sighed. "I should have guessed as much."

"Great. The dungeon." He lowered the ball. "It's bound to be guarded."

She shook her head. "Probably not. A key should suffice to keep Mr. Matheson here."

"But why is he in the dungeon?"

"I suspect that Count Erdel can answer that, Kyler."

There was a peremptory knock at the door. "That'll be Arpad," she said. Hastily, she returned their linguachip settings to Romanian.

* * *

The ubiquitous Arpad served the food in a large dining room, the table measuring about fifteen feet by three. Walls were adorned with ancient crests and weapons, many draped with cobwebs. A blazing fire in the hearth at either end of the room barely managed to warm the place. Candles offered minimal light. Shadows hovered in niches all around.

The meal consisted of soup that seemed reluctant to slide down Kyler's throat: greasy liquid floating with tripe, carrots, turnip, celery and beef hock, their hostess proudly informed him. Not for the first time he wondered how Tertia coped with the ingestion of organic food; it's not as if she imbibed oil or power cells. Maybe her insides burned the food and converted it to electric energy; he must ask her. The second course was slightly more palatable: potato goulash with smoked meat. This was accompanied by truly delicious sweetbread.

When the next course arrived, he wondered how Lady Lilith managed to retain her sylph-like shape. The grilled sausage was called "mici" by Lilith and comprised ground beef, pork and mutton, flavored with black pepper and hot paprika. A side-dish of mustard was offered, should they not find it spicy enough.

"The mici are delectable," Tertia observed, wiping her mouth with the red linen serviette. "Though I thought the garlic flavoring was lacking."

Lilith nodded and smiled, though it appeared more like a grimace. "Garlic is prevalent in the area but it does not agree with our constitution. So, you have eaten Romanian food before?"

"I have tasted the cuisine of most countries. It's a hobby of mine."

Kyler wondered if Tertia was lying. The allusion to garlic was not lost on him, however, and he hastened to change the subject, chuckling and grabbing his belly as Arpad entered with another laden tray. "Oh, and here's another course."

"Ah, my favorite," Lilith exclaimed, clapping her hands. "Papanash. It's made from sweet cow cheese. You can try it with one of the preserves." She indicated the small jars of marmalade and jam and a bowl of powdered sugar.

"You are too generous, Lady Lilith," Kyler said, resisting a groan.

* * *

Chief Inspector Irving slowly recovered his breath after the climb to this second floor. Energy conservation monitors had long ago banned out-dome elevator use. He stood outside the apartment door, leaning on his stick, while Damon rang the bell. Five of the eight corridor lights were broken, but there was adequate illumination.

"Still no response," Irving stated.

"Do you want to look the other way?" Damon asked, producing from his jacket a small electronic disc.

"I'm investigating several murders, Mr. Cole. I've left my scruples in the car."

"Good." Damon pressed the end of the disc against the door-lock and it emitted a high-pitched whistle. The lock clicked open.

"I'll go first," Irving said, and limped inside with the aid of his stick. He flicked on the lights which lit up the hallway.

On their left were two doors, and three on their right.

A faint humming sound filled the apartment. "What's that?" Irving asked.

Damon shrugged his broad shoulders. "Maybe a wonky refrigerator—or a Zygma projector …?"

"We'd better find out, then, Mr. Cole."

The first on the right opened into a lounge graced with low-slung streamlined furniture—ideal for aerodynamic flight but it appeared as uncomfortable as hell, Damon mused.

"What's that smell?" he whispered as Irving joined him at a closed door leading from the lounge.

Damon opened the door and was hit by a wave of warm slightly putrid air. The room was spacious with a huge black leather ottoman sofa in the center. Stationed behind the sofa were six radiant-heat lamps, glowing redly.

"He takes his historical studies seriously," Damon said. "This must be Matheson's study." Along two walls were bookcases crammed with books, mostly hardbacks. On one wall hung an assortment of weapons—a dirk, a kris, a spear, a halberd, a broadsword, a Roman legionnaire's shield, a medieval mace. "And he believes in the fables, it seems." A couple of shelves harbored several pointed stakes made from sturdy ash, a mallet, and a satin-lined box, nestling within six silver bullets and a Smith & Wesson revolver.

They stepped towards the ottoman and Irving let out a gasp.

On the floor behind the sofa lay a man and two women fully clothed in black, supine on top of a mixture of dark soil and straw; fungi sprouted between them.

Irving swore under his breath. "I've heard of cannabis farms in bedrooms, but growing vampires?"

Damon glanced at the window: the black blind was drawn. "They're not growing them, Inspector. They're resting. If myths have any credence, they'll be rising any time soon now it's night."

"What do we do about them?"

"We haven't come equipped to deal with vampires, so we must leave them for the moment and investigate the other rooms. Our priority is finding Matheson."

Giving a shudder, Irving added, "Well, Mr. Cole, I hope there are no more of those creatures lurking."

"Me, too, Inspector."

They left, shutting the door, and crossed the hall to the room opposite. This was a standard bedroom, strangely incongruous in contrast. The adjacent room was the kitchen; opposite this was a dining room. The next door opened onto a room that only contained a long table, its surface filled with a viewscreen, a contraption of rods, assorted plates and injection devices, and next to it was a bulky yet familiar machine.

"And there it is," Damon said.

Tom Matheson's Zygma projector was humming faintly, its faceted eyes winking randomly.

"What does that mean?" Irving asked.

"Somebody—presumably Matheson—is currently using it." Damon checked the papers on a nearby table, and then the dials on the projector. "There's no clue as to the destination of the jump."

"From what we've learned so far, we can make a reasonable guess."

Damon scrutinized the contraption on the table. "It's a 3D printer." He held up three ornate brooches, each with a red button that glowed. "Matheson has manufactured recall beacons." He frowned. "But why so many?"

The humming stopped. The sudden silence weighed heavily on Damon. He lowered the brooches to the table top.

In front of the projector two shapes shimmered into their reality, and transformed into two men. Neither of them resembled the historian Tom Matheson.

7

Pleading tiredness and explaining they were anxious to wake early to return to their coach and coachman on the morrow, Tertia and Kyler climbed the stairs to their room.

Once inside, with the door closed on their escort Arpad, Kyler turned to Tertia. "We've got to get inside that dungeon tonight."

Crouching down, Tertia peeked through the keyhole. "There's a key inserted, so I can't see." She tried the door, but it was locked. "The tumblers are well oiled, I didn't hear him lock it."

"At least something works well in this decrepit place." He grimaced. "That food was awful."

"Of its type, actually, it wasn't too bad. I've tasted worse."

"Oh, about you eating …"

She held up a hand. "We haven't got time for that now. Come."

Tertia strode over to the window, opened it. "We'll get out this way."

"But we're at least two floors up, and without a ladder."

"We'll just improvise." She turned to eye the bed. "The traditional methods will suffice."

"You must be joking. Knotted sheets?"

"Why not?"

The sheets reached well below the window of a room directly below theirs. With difficulty, Kyler found purchase for his feet on the window sill and steadied himself. Tertia handed him a knife from her satchel and he winkled the window latch open.

They slid inside and jumped to the floor. The room was unlit, but a faint glow shone under the door.

Kyler tried the door and found it unlocked.

Treading with care, they stepped onto a landing.

No sound. Anywhere.

Wall torches flickered, casting shadows about.

Nobody was around, it seemed.

Kyler led, moving to the head of the staircase.

They descended swiftly, glad of the shadows.

Directed by Tertia holding her slimfone, he hurried across the vestibule to a door to the left of the front entrance porch. It was unlocked. A small landing and then stairs going down.

He heard faint murmuring.

He took out his Remington revolver and noticed Tertia was already holding her .45. It crossed his mind that he hadn't loaded any silver bullets. Or were they only effective against werewolves? God knows—and He ain't telling.

The stone floor at the base of the stairs was littered with dried scraps of animal bones; mostly chicken, Kyler reckoned.

Flies buzzed; they seemed everywhere.

Over to the right was an open doorway, and a lambent light glowed through. On the left was another door, but that was shut, with a small barred window opening.

"Carmilla, time for you to drink your fill," said Lilith. He recognized her voice, though it sounded sultry now. "Don't be greedy, leave him alive."

Cocking the revolver, Kyler stepped into the doorway and gasped.

Wrists shackled and hanging by chains fixed to the stone wall, a fair-haired man with a prominent Roman nose groaned plaintively. It must be Tom Matheson.

On either side of Matheson stood two women, both of them in diaphanous carmine night-attire.

Matheson's eyes were shut, his features pale. His once-white shirt was torn in several places, revealing a hirsute torso. Blood stained his hairy chest, shirt and trousers. Lady Lilith stood on his left, the other one, presumably Carmilla, was leaning toward Matheson, her mouth open wide, her long blonde tresses draped like tendrils to her shoulders.

* * *

Irving and Damon stared.

"Who the hell are you?" Damon demanded. His allusion to "hell" seemed horribly apt.

The first man was cadaverous, his hair dark streaked with gray, his high forehead glistening with sweat, the hairline pointed to a peak. His eyes were deeply sunk, blazing red, and his lips were swollen, engorged, while his cheekbones appeared capable of slitting throats. He wore a black frock coat, a white shirt and a cravat pinned with a brooch.

The other man was slight of build, slightly stooped, with close-set darting black eyes and a porcine nose. He too wore a cravat and brooch.

Clearly, Damon mused, they've just activated their recall beacons.

"Ah, you must be an acquaintance of Mr. Matheson," the first man said, speaking English with a thick accent.

"You haven't answered my question," Damon snapped.

"I am Count Erdel and this is my associate Emil Blaga." He offered a mocking bow.

"You've come for your three vampires, is that it?" Damon said.

"Oh, no. I intend leaving Bran, Demetra and Ilinca here to recruit more unfortunate souls. I have simply brought Emil here to boost their numbers and accelerate the process." Erdel chuckled and pointed behind Irving. "I believe you've seen them already, no?"

Damon pivoted on his heel.

The three vampires from the other room approached the doorway, blocking off their escape.

The male and two females stood, adoring eyes upon the count. Soil dropped from their clothing; Damon could see a trail of earth behind them. The male's skin was blue-tinged, his thin mouth pouted, sucking in air that didn't seem to find his lungs; his chest was still, while his bony hands trembled at his sides, the nails yellow and long. The two females could have been twins, wearing long flowing black taffeta skirts and tight-fitting black leather basques that emphasized their bosoms; their lips were narrow, bloodless, their visages ugly. One was blonde with black streaks, the other had long flowing black hair streaked with white.

"Bran," the count said, addressing the male, "please dispose of the old man."

"Old man," Irving exclaimed in an affronted tone.

"Ilinca," Count Erdel said to the blonde, "you can drink of the muscular one."

"With great pleasure."

"What about me?" Demetra moaned.

"You can watch. I'm sure Ilinca will save some blood for you."

Foolishly, Damon hadn't thought to bring a weapon. It's not as if he was on a time-jump. He was in the here and now.

Cackling obscenely, Bran attacked Irving, his fingers bent like claws, his jaw wide, displaying pointed incisors and a furred tongue.

Irving took a step back and then, gripping his walking stick like a small spear, he charged forward to meet his attacker.

Bran didn't seem alarmed as Irving thrust the end of the stick into his chest. Then, an instant later his face reflected intense agony and he stared down at the wood protruding from his undead torso. "Hawthorn! Curse you, it's made of hawthorn!"

Puzzled, Damon had no time to linger. The two women rushed him. He ran towards them then at the last second dropped to the floor and rolled into their shins, tripping both.

He continued to roll, reached the doorway and scrambled to his feet. Following the trail of soil, he raced to the study.

Damon burst in, his senses beset by the earthy smell and the wave of radiant-heat.

Unexpectedly a massive force and weight on his back and neck propelled him forward, tumbling into the ottoman. One of the women was on his back, snarling, slavering at his neck. He rolled, slammed her body between the sofa and his own. It was the blonde, Ilinca. She let go and he scrambled off her, righted himself and ran to the shelf. He grabbed a wooden stake from the display as the blonde pounced again. She grinned, her breath rancid on his face, as she lowered her fangs to his neck.

Then her grin became a grimace.

Imbedded in her chest was the stake. He thrust harder, deeper.

Her evil eyes were accusing, and then clouded. She went limp and slithered down his body to the floor.

Grabbing the other stake and the mallet, Damon stepped over Ilinca's corpse and came face-to-face with the other woman, Demetra.

"Demetra, come with us—now," the count shouted.

Trembling at sight of her fallen companion, Demetra hesitated. She eyed the stake in Damon's hand and swerved round, raced towards the projector room.

The humming sound started up again.

By the time Damon reached the room, the Zygma projector was flashing, and the three shapes were shimmering, becoming indistinct. Irving sat with his back against the wall, bruised but otherwise unhurt. Lying next to him was the body of Bran.

"Erdel threw me against the wall and then escaped with Emil and Demetra," Irving said. "I couldn't stop them."

* * *

"Stop!" Kyler barked, levelling his revolver.

Lilith flinched and turned to face him, while Carmilla hesitated then pressed her mouth to the man's neck.

Kyler fired a shot over their heads; the slug hit the brick and ricocheted around the cell, echoing.

Tertia bellowed, "Do as he says, Carmilla." She stood beside him, gun aimed.

Carmilla stopped and slowly turned her head and looked at them both, scowling, her mouth dribbling red.

"I'm disappointed in the pair of you," Lilith said, "after I've been so hospitable."

"Are these two our new invigorating supply?" Carmilla wheezed.

Lilith licked her lips. "That was my intention."

"Sorry to disappoint you," Kyler stated. "Now, step away from him." He jerked the handgun.

Letting out a sneering laugh, Lilith placed her hands on her hips. "What are you going to do, shoot us?"

"If you don't do as I say, yes." Out of the corner of his eye, he noticed Tertia had removed her fob watch.

115

"You have a pressing engagement, my dear?" Lilith queried, and then, not waiting for an answer, she leapt at Kyler.

He fired almost point blank at her. The force of the bullet slowed Lilith for an instant, but then she hit him with all her weight, slashed her fingernails at his face, and scrambled over him as he fell to the floor, his shoulders hitting bruisingly hard.

There was a blur of carmine, and then Lilith was past him and gone.

Carmilla screamed.

Raising himself on one elbow, he saw Tertia brandish her fob-watch laser; the beam sliced into Carmilla's neck.

The undead woman's head toppled, spraying very little blood, and hit the floor seconds before its body.

"Bullets won't work," Tertia said.

"Evidently," Kyler said, his hand coming away bloody from his scratched face.

They rushed over to the chained Matheson. He was still breathing.

Tertia went back to Carmilla's corpse, rummaged through her skirts. "Damn. She hasn't got the keys."

"Over there," Kyler called, pointing to a hook near the door.

She took them and unlocked the shackles from Matheson's wrists.

Matheson toppled into Kyler's arms. For a second they stood there, and then Matheson opened his green-gray eyes. "Water …"

On a rickety wooden table was a pitcher with a ladle and water. Tertia went over and sniffed it. "It's potable." She ladled some into Matheson's mouth.

Finally, Matheson was able to stand with support from Kyler, though he wobbled a little. "A bit unsteady, haven't used my legs in a long while." He grimaced. "Can we get out of here? Please?"

"Sure," Kyler said.

Supporting Matheson, the pair moved up the stairs and out into the vestibule. There was no sign of Lilith or Arpad.

They went to the lounge where they'd first met Lilith.

Nobody here, either.

Gratefully, Matheson sat on a settee. Tertia went to the drinks cabinet and poured a good measure of red wine.

"I'll have one of those as well," Kyler said. "You?"

"No, I have no need to be polite. I have sufficient sustenance."

She brought two full glasses. Kyler sipped his while Matheson took the glass from her and gulped half its contents. "Thanks. I needed that."

While Tertia kept watch on the door, Matheson told them how he'd been taken prisoner by Count Erdel. He was tortured into revealing details about the Zygma projector. "He left me with his two women to feast on me. They drank enough to sustain them, but kept me alive … a living death, I fear."

"You're contaminated?" Tertia queried.

Matheson shook his head. "I don't know. I fear as much, though."

"And Erdel used your recall device?" Kyler asked.

"Yes. Erdel saw his chance to travel to our time, his future, where superstition is dead, where nobody believes in vampires. He gloated, telling me about his plans. He'd prey on them. His victims would be unsuspecting."

"But why?" Kyler demanded.

"He's lonely. He wants to increase the numbers of the undead. He took with him a small crate of Transylvanian earth from the castle grounds to contaminate the soil in his future. Soil conducive to vampires."

"What about Lilith and Carmilla?"

"He promised to return for them."

"We should get you back to our time now," Kyler said. "You need urgent medical attention."

Tertia shook her head. "But he needs his recall beacon to go back …"

"Matheson, what's your beacon look like?"

"It's a brooch; it fastened on my cravat …"

At that moment, the air in the room made a crackling sound. Kyler had heard it before; incipient Zygma particles coalescing, announcing a time-jump.

8

"It must be done," Damon said, removing the broadsword from Matheson's study wall.

"Unpleasant, but I agree." Irving closed a hardbound book entitled *Vampyres*, one from Matheson's extensive library.

Damon swung the sword blade down, severing the head of Ilinca from its body.

"I'm surprised," Irving said. "I expected blood to spurt …"

"Me too. Then again, the heart had stopped pumping …"

"True. You know, I think Charlie, our pathologist, would find it interesting to study the vampire physiology. How can they be dead yet function? Their brains clearly work, and they're still capable of movement, yet they're supposed to be dead …"

"She's welcome to them," Damon said and went to the Zygma projector room.

Irving followed and was in time to see Damon behead Bran.

"Having skimmed that book," Irving said, "I now know that my hawthorn walking stick definitely didn't agree with him."

"And according to that same book, the ash tree is lethal as well, and beheading makes sure they don't rise again."

"Perish the thought," Irving shuddered, and then his slimfone trilled. He answered it, listened and replied, "We'll come at once. Stay calm, Charlie."

Damon wiped the sword on Bran's clothing. "Charlie? Was that—?"

"Yes, our pathologist at the morgue." He shook his head in dismay. "She says four of the corpses have run off and she's locked the fifth in the cold room."

"Run off?"

Irving shrugged. "They must have become vampires." He beckoned for Damon to follow him. "We'd better get there pronto."

On their way to the street, Damon said, "But that means if vampires run wild, they'll infect the entire population ..."

"Possibly. Remember, though, the normal destination for corpses whose families can afford it is the crematorium—situated *outside* the dome." Indeed, that white ash contributed to the grime on the Plexiglas dome. "Burial is reserved for the super-rich in their mausoleums—*inside* the dome."

"Yes, but for those who can't afford the crematorium, Count Erdel is ideally placed since outside the bubble the dead are often interred in common graves, lying there for undead resurrection."

Here, out-dome, any newly dead infected with a vampire's DNA would rise up as night cloaked the land. Damon shuddered at the thought of a plague of the undead.

* * *

As three shapes transformed into people in front of the Zygma projector, Tom Matheson stood unsteadily, his pale face draining to an alabaster shade. "Oh, God, it's Count Erdel," he exclaimed.

Kyler and Tertia stepped in front of Matheson, taking a defensive stance.

"Who are the other two?" Kyler asked.

"I don't know," Matheson croaked, his voice tremulous.

"Damn you, Matheson. I should have let them kill you." Erdel glared at Kyler and Tertia, their blood-spattered clothing. "What have you done with Carmilla and Lilith?"

"Tertia," Kyler shouted, "take the count, I'll go for the other man."

Tertia's laser beam blasted.

Count Erdel had half-turned, flourishing his cape, and the laser sliced away a portion of the cape and cut into the count's shoulder. He yelped and stepped back in alarm. "Demetra, the door—quick," he called to the woman.

At the same time, Kyler leapt to land on a chair that stood against the wall and pulled free a basket-hilted sword from its display hook. In one swift motion, he swiveled round and threw the sword at the other man.

"Emil, watch out," Erdel cried, rushing to Demetra's side at the doorway.

Too late: the man called Emil staggered as the sword penetrated his chest.

The woman hissed like a snake and backed off.

As Emil sank to his knees, Erdel urged, "Come, Demetra, we must flee."

Tertia ran to Emil and unhesitatingly beheaded him with her laser. "Another one down," she said.

Kyler pulled the sword free. "But where are Lilith and Arpad?"

"They could be, anywhere." She pointed to the corpse at their feet. "We now have a recall beacon for Matheson." She knelt and plucked the brooch from the blood-soaked cravat.

"Yes, but this beacon will transport the wearer to Matheson's machine, not ours."

"Matheson needs medical aid, which will be more available in the dome," Tertia said. "You should go with him, and I'll use his recall beacon to return to his machine."

"There's no telling what you'll find at his end."

"I'll take my chances. Anyway, I'll be more likely to handle whatever I encounter there."

"Your logic's unassailable."

Tertia handed him her reticule. "I'll make my way back to the nearest dome gate."

"Well, be careful …"

"Of course." She clasped the brooch beacon. "Don't delay. Activate now."

And then she shimmered and was gone.

Carrying his sword, Kyler hurried to Matheson who lay prostrate on the settee.

"Here, take this," he said, proffering Tertia's reticule. "It's a recall beacon, it will take you to Continuity's machine."

Docilely, Matheson took the small bag.

"No, you won't take him," screamed Lilith.

Swiveling on his heel, Kyler raised his sword.

Lilith stood at the doorway, Arpad behind her. Her face twisted in anger and she charged across the room. Close on her heels came Arpad brandishing an axe.

She was unarmed. But he had no qualms about killing her. How do you kill someone who has already been killed? Beheading. Tertia was accomplished at that with her laser. Surgical, almost.

Kyler swung the sword back and forth to dissuade Lilith.

"Leave him," Lilith shouted hoarsely, stopping out of reach of Kyler's blade. "He will soon be one of us anyway."

"No, he comes back with us."

Abruptly, the full weight of Matheson descended on Kyler's shoulders, sent him sprawling at Lilith's feet.

Snuffling and snarling, Matheson's fingers were like talons, plucking at Kyler's jacket and shirt, tearing the fabric. His breath was foul, sickening. Matheson's spittle drooled on Kyler's face.

"See, he is already one of us," Lilith exulted.

Gripping the sword handle, Kyler rolled and rolled, away from Lilith, trying in vain to shake Matheson from his back. He glimpsed Arpad standing nearby, clasping the axe, a smile on his face.

Exerting himself, Kyler slammed his head backwards, and felt it connect with the bone of Matheson's face. The historian's grip slackened and Kyler took advantage, wrenching free, twisting away.

Kyler raised himself on one knee as Arpad ran towards him, axe raised.

Thrusting himself forward, he gripped the sword two-handed and sliced at Arpad's legs, and literally cut one of them from under him.

Screeching loudly, Arpad tumbled sideways, the axe clattering to the floor.

Kyler righted himself, got to one knee, and saw Matheson lying dazed on the floor. Then Lilith snatched the reticule from Matheson's hand. She pressed the button and shimmered and was gone.

Damn!

Steeling himself, Kyler ran to Matheson and without hesitation beheaded the historian.

Arpad groaned, trying to fix his severed limb to its stump, oblivious of the blood that gushed. Maybe this was the same Arpad from the letter; maybe it wasn't. Faithful retainer or immortal vampire?

"Let me put you out of your misery," Kyler said, and did.

Trembling with the after-shock of his near-demise and the carnage around him, Kyler pressed the recall button on his snuffbox.

* * *

"I see you've come prepared," Charlie said, nodding at Damon's broadsword.

"I can assure you, it's effective," Irving told her, grasping his walking stick firmly. "Ready when you are."

Charlie bit her lip pensively, and then fingered the keypad. The refrigeration door hissed as the seal unlocked. She heaved it open.

Damon rushed through, slashing left and right with the sword, in case the vampire had been lurking on either side.

He felt foolish when he realized she was directly in front of him.

The undead woman stood draped in a white sheet, staring. Slowly, her lips curled back, revealing fangs, and her eyes lit up. She licked her lips and walked towards him, arms outstretched, like a lover welcoming him, the sheet falling to the floor.

Those eyes mesmerized him. His hands felt so heavy, he could hardly hold the sword. He let it clang to the floor.

Her eyes glowed red. Inflamed.

His mind was no longer his own. He welcomed her embrace.

"Get back, you bitch," Irving shouted and rushed in front of Damon, wielding his walking stick.

The woman hesitated, unsure.

The eye-connection was broken and Damon shook himself awake. He shuddered, aware that his mind had been hijacked, even if only fleetingly.

The two of them circled the woman. Both now avoided looking into her eyes.

She turned, snarling, facing Irving one moment, then Damon the next.

"On three, go in for the kill," Irving said.

"Right," Damon replied. "One."

"Two."

"Caine, help," Charlie shouted.

They both looked back at the doorway. The corpses of two of the earlier victims stood there dressed in male clothing, blood dribbling down chins.

"They're wearing Hodge's clothes," Charlie called, backing into the room. She grabbed a chair next to the desk, used it to ward off their advance.

The naked undead woman shrieked and leaped on Irving's back, her thin arms encircling his neck.

"Get her off me before she bites!"

9

When Kyler materialized in the prop-laden hotel vestibule, he crouched, long sword held ready and eyes wary. The gut-wrenching pain of the time-jump eased as he scanned his surroundings.

He felt a mixture of relief and annoyance, to find that Lilith wasn't here.

Before making a move, he crossed over to the portable Zygma projector. It seemed an age since Damon had wheeled it in. He locked the recalibration wheels so that should Lilith return, she couldn't time-jump anywhere.

Then he walked cautiously from the theatrical flats to the office.

Lilith was nowhere. And there was no sign of any disturbance.

He checked the windows; it was night, so there was nobody else here now.

An eerie silence pervaded the place.

If Lilith was free to roam, she would create new vampires at her leisure, supping blood to her heart's content. How long would it take for the entire population of London dome to become infected? It would be exponential, of course. He shook his head; he couldn't do the arithmetic.

Then he spotted Tertia's reticule on the floor, near the exit door. He knelt to pick it up. His heart seemed to stumble and his stomach lurched as he wondered how she was faring in Matheson's apartment. Living in the dome, it was easy to forget how precarious life could be outside. Millions lived there, and got through every day, somehow, without the cossetting supplied by the dome system. But there were ugly and dangerous things out-dome. He feared for her, and then shook himself. She was an android, not a real woman.

* * *

Clasping her laser in readiness, Tertia materialized in Matheson's projector room and was confronted with a beheaded male corpse on the floor. Must be Damon and Irving's work, she surmised. She hastily scanned her surroundings. It was all clear.

Erdel and Demetra would have arrived earlier, and obviously hadn't lingered.

Warily, she checked out the other rooms in the apartment, but there was no sign of the two escaped vampires. She did find another headless corpse, though: a female in the study. Here too she spotted the Smith & Wesson revolver and silver bullets and thrust them into her shoulder-bag; her research suggested that the

127

bullets wouldn't be fatal to vampires, only werewolves, but they'd still cause severe damage.

Aiming her laser at the Zygma projector, she burned and slashed, destroying it beyond conceivable repair. Erdel wouldn't be able to use it again.

Burnt cable and metal lingering in her olfactory senses, she gingerly left the apartment and shut the door. The corridor lighting was dismal, so she amplified her visual acuity to penetrate shadows.

She attuned her hearing, listening for any stealthy movement on either side as she passed the doors of other apartments. The place was strangely silent; no radio, no music, no television.

Next to the elevators halfway down the corridor she saw a fire extinguisher on the wall and a sign stating, "Lifts Out of Order." The fire exit stairs were at the end of the corridor.

She was about halfway along when several doors on either side opened at the same time, as if coordinated.

Vampires stood in the doorways uttering a low hiss.

The fire door ahead slid open and two men entered the corridor; shaved heads, multiple scar tissue, and blood-soaked clothes. Vampires as well.

So, Count Erdel's contagion had spread already.

"Looking for us?" Erdel enquired from behind.

Tertia pivoted.

He stepped out of one of the rooms she'd passed. By his side was the woman, Demetra.

"Just you by yourself, all alone?" Demetra smirked. "What a shame."

Before she could reach for the Smith & Wesson revolver, two males rushed her from each side, grabbed her upper arms and held her firmly.

"Keep her still," Erdel whispered hoarsely, his tone suffused with desire. He came closer as one of her captors pressed her head back, baring her throat.

10

Moments of lucid thought for Nevil Hodge came less frequently, but this was one such. He lay on his bed, weak, depleted of much blood. His bare chest was spattered; they'd expressed no sexual desire so he still wore his pajama pants. Two of the blood-suckers had gone to the morgue. "We must free our companion," One had said; she'd ransacked Nevil's wardrobe and taken Three with her.

Now, Two and Four sat on either side of him on the bed, their lips full, gorged. They were not asleep. "Vampires sleep during the day," Four had told him. "So, we will tie you up then." But they were definitely in a state of narcosis.

Surprisingly clearheaded, he eased himself to foot of the bed. His breathing was shallow, his head dizzy. When clear of their feet, he rolled quietly onto the carpeted floor.

Christ, he was weak.

He wanted to lie here, just lie still and rest.

No, he must deal with these creatures.

Slowly, on hands and elbows, he crawled towards the bathroom. The coldness of the tiles invigorated him slightly. He grabbed the wall towel rail and pulled himself to his feet.

He found the can of air freshener on top of the toilet cistern.

It was a struggle, but finally he gripped the canister under his arm and used both hands to pull off the lid.

Exhausted at this effort, he leaned against the wall and sucked in air. Carefully, he thrust the aerosol in his left pocket.

He wondered how long he could remain conscious. Usually, after they fed off him, he lapsed into a nightmare-filled sleep.

He feared he didn't have long. They might regain consciousness any minute. Or One and Three might return; he had no way of knowing how long they'd been away already.

He wondered if they'd driven his car to the morgue. He supposed the skills of their dead hosts might be transferable. They wouldn't like the oncoming headlights, he reckoned.

Enough of this time-wasting, he berated himself.

He shuffled his bare feet across the floor and reached the carpet of the bedroom.

Now, the kitchen.

It was a long way off.

Finally, an age later, he reached the kitchen and worked his way round the counter top to the gas cooker. In the second drawer down, he found the box of matches and put them in his right pocket, then slowly made his way back to the bedroom.

Sweating, weak, he sank to his knees. The sound of his landing seemed very loud. Four stirred and then turned on her side, snorting.

He crawled to the other side of the bed and heaved himself upright.

Looking down on the pair, his stomach turned.

Slowly, carefully, he extracted the aerosol canister and then the box of matches. Holding his breath, he struck a match alight and then pressed the nozzle, aiming the spray at the nearest vampire, Two. As she woke suddenly, eyes starting, coughing on the spray and perfume, he put the match to the spray.

Immediately, it was a blow-torch and Two's face was on fire. She screeched, an eldritch call that almost chilled what blood he had left.

Four turned over, murmured something sleepily and he blasted her with the flame too.

Frantically, trying to maintain his stance, he kept aiming the torch-flames at the two shrieking vampires. Neither seemed capable of rising from the bed. His nostrils filled with singed hair and skin. He wanted to vomit, but he had no stomach contents to void.

He prayed he had enough of the aerosol to immolate them to the point where they wouldn't return from the dead.

* * *

While Charlie fended off the two vampires with a chair, Damon swung the sword blade at the back of the attacking woman's legs. It flinched as the tendons were cut but maintained its grip on Irving, the legs now dangling useless.

Snagging the fallen sheet, Damon jumped on the back of the undead woman. He wrapped the sheet round his left forearm and slid the sword blade under her chin, then used his protected forearm and sword hand to heave back hard. He felt the blade cut into the throat, sever the cartilage and finally decapitate the vampire.

Splashed with her blood, he fell back with the head and torso.

Freed at last, Irving didn't hesitate but charged the two vampires threatening Charlie.

His walking stick penetrated the flesh and pierced a heart.

The second vampire smashed the chair, threw it aside and lunged for Charlie.

It met the bloody blade of Damon's sword.

Panting for breath, Irving hugged Charlie. "Are you all right?" he wheezed.

"Yes, Caine. But—your neck …"

Damon examined it. "No puncture, just bruising and scratches."

"Thank God for that," Charlie said.

"And," Irving added, "hawthorn and cold steel …"

11

The vampire on Tertia's right stank of cannabis; his clothing reeked of it: a bad habit of the human before he became one of the undead. The back of her hand knocked against his jacket pocket. A lighter, she reckoned; no longer needed by its transformed owner.

Tertia was forced to look down her nose at Erdel. He licked thin dark lips. "I'm going to enjoy this. Repayment for interfering and depriving us of Matheson and poor dear Carmilla." He bit into her offered neck.

Seconds later he jolted backwards and spat out some of her blood. "What is that?" he spluttered.

Her two captors were momentarily distracted and relaxed their hold.

Tertia pulled out the lighter and turned its wheel high and ignited it, flashing the flame in the nearest captor's face. Emitting a high-pitched shriek, he let go immediately and she swung round, burning the second vampire.

The lighter flame persisted and she flashed it at Erdel, but he backed away.

Suddenly, she swung round and attacked the male vampire in the doorway to her right.

She charged at him and he slunk to one side, cowering. She rushed into the apartment and kicked the door shut behind her.

A lounge with doors leading off; all the doors were open. The kitchen was on the left. She ran inside, spotted a window above the sink. Grabbing a stool, she smashed the glass, peered out into the night. The window overlooked the road; there was an unlit street light about five feet away, directly opposite.

She heard the door collapse to the onslaught of the vampires.

She switched on all of the gas stove's knobs. Within seconds, she smelled the pungent gas.

Perched on the windowsill, she waited.

A minute later by the wall clock, two vampires entered. She heard others ransacking the apartment's rooms. One of them saw her and snarled.

Tertia lit the lighter and threw it at the stove and in the same instant pivoted and jumped.

She caught the post of the street light and slid down.

Before her feet hit the ground, the apartment exploded.

The majority of street lights were either not working or broken. Shadows loomed everywhere.

Her enhanced vision was unimpaired by poor lighting so she saw the two vampires emerge from the back of the apartment block and run towards her. Standing still, she waited. On they came, slavering, whimpering. Perhaps they felt the demise of their brethren?

When they were both within three feet of her, she pulled out the Smith & Wesson and fired into their gaping mouths.

They juddered to a halt, limbs twitching in shock.

A silver bullet wouldn't kill them, but it would incapacitate them long enough to allow her to decapitate the creatures with her laser.

Leaving the bodies and severed heads where they lay, Tertia turned right and strolled along the path, heading in a northerly direction. Constantly alert.

The streets were littered with garbage and derelict vehicles. The local authority armed response teams maintained adequate passage through most roadways, using bulldozers, but it was an ongoing problem as resources diminished and vehicles were abandoned or looters took cars to joyride to destruction. The citizens living in the domes were protected; in their bubble, they remained ignorant of the state of the country outside. Surprisingly, the country functioned after a fashion. She knew that the rest of Europe was even worse.

She passed the dilapidated Railway public house; it had never recovered from the demise of the rail system. This road was signposted as the B212; a few driverless vehicles passed in both directions, windows blanked. Over on the other side of the road a derelict electric bus number 202 leaned against a building's wall.

Further on, she noticed a cluster of people standing around a brazier, its coals red-hot. She wrapped her hand round the revolver in her satchel. They looked normal homeless people, not vampires.

In a short while she reached Shooters Hill gas station, where she found an abandoned hybrid car. She opened the engine cowling and examined the innards. A minor wiring fault, nothing serious, which took ten minutes to fix. The charge and fuel registered full. She got in and motored away.

After many dead ends, roads blocked by burnt out wrecks, collapsed walls and felled trees, she drove onto the Old Kent Road and headed west.

She passed buildings daubed with graffiti from several nationalities; "multicultural filth," the deceased prime minister had called it.

The closer she approached the center of London, the busier the streets appeared. People ventured out, shopped, chatted, even though it was night. Her vehicle's sensors detected laughter sometimes. No vampires here, then. Maybe that explosion had accounted for them?

She had no doubt she could obtain access through the dome's western gate.

It surprised her, but she found she was concerned for Kyler. Next, she'd be dreaming about him instead of electric sheep, she mused, and laughed.

* * *

Lilith was unfamiliar with the modern surroundings. The sky was closed, a kind of solid thing, arching above her. Vehicles without horses passed, women wore strange and quite brazen clothing, people of all shades talked into small hand-held contraptions, and there was constant noise wherever she turned.

Her one consolation was that there was plenty of blood available. And the people seemed disconnected, many not even acknowledging her presence among them, too busy communing with those objects in their hands.

She wondered if she would find her husband in this strange world. Tears formed. She missed him already.

First, though, she needed to drink blood. That meant she had to have somewhere private where she wouldn't be detected. Somewhere reasonably familiar.

12

It was past midnight when they had their reunion at Continuity Inc. Kyler embraced Tertia and hugged her tight.

"You seem like you're pleased to be together," observed Damon, arms akimbo.

Then, slightly embarrassed, Kyler relinquished his hold.

Inspector Irving entered holding Dr. Charlotte Thornley's hand. "We found Nevil Hodge at home," Irving told them. "He dealt with the stray two vampire victims and he is now hospitalized, restrained and being monitored."

"And," Tertia added, "I can only assume Count Erdel perished in the explosion I mentioned."

"So," Damon said, "we've only got Lilith unaccounted for, is that right?"

"I think so," Kyler replied. "I'm sorry I couldn't find her."

Tertia gave him a hug. "You forget, I've got the 'speckled ball thing.'"

"The Zygma particle detector," Kyler said.

"Yes." She delved in her satchel and brought it out. "I'll have to recalibrate it to ignore all of us here. Fortunately, all the particles it registers have jump date time tags."

A map of London was produced and within five minutes they had pinpointed a single suspect. "That suggests that the count died, after all," Tertia observed.

"If this 'speckle' is Lilith, where is she?" Kyler asked.

"It seems most fitting," Tertia said. "She's at Madame Tussauds in the Chamber of Horrors ..."

Damon chuckled. "She won't enjoy trying to suck those waxworks dry."

"I'd like to capture her alive," Dr. Thornley said. "If that's not a paradox."

"We can try." Irving gave a slight shudder. "Though as you recall, at close quarters a female vampire is a terrible thing."

"We could learn a lot from her physiology, you know."

"I'm convinced," Irving said. "Let's make a couple of calls, Damon."

* * *

They made their way in the driverless Mercedes, part of a convoy also comprising a half-dozen police officers in black riot wagons.

The museum had been secured since rioting in the area two months ago. But it soon became obvious that an entry had been forced. Flashlights blazing, they scoured the building, finally arriving at the basement entrance to the Chamber of Horrors.

Heads of Dr. Crippen, Adolf Hitler, and Genghis Khan rolled about on the floor, their necks pierced and torn. Lilith was cursing as she wrestled with the effigy of Vlad the Impaler.

As she heard them enter, she swung round, fangs bared but bloodless. Tears streaked down her face.

"She looks quite frustrated," Irving observed. Then he directed his men to act.

Two burly policemen threw a heavy mesh net over Lilith. Her shoulders slumped and she didn't fight as they tightly wound it round her.

"Take her to the morgue," Dr. Thornley said. "We'll restrain her and then feed her, keep her alive— or whatever state she's in."

On their return, Kyler said, "You know, we've been so wrapped up in worrying about history, we haven't really considered the state of the present."

"I know," Tertia said. "It's in a bit of a mess, isn't it?"

"Do you think another branch of Continuity Inc is right now in the future, trying to fix us?"

Tertia shrugged. "I don't know." She held his hand. "I rather like us as we are."

✝

ABOUT THE AUTHOR

Nik has been writing for over 50 years and believes he's getting the hang of it now. Sold his first short story in 1971 and over 100 since, plus many articles, cartoons and illustrations. His first book sale didn't happen until 2007—quite a long wait, he reckons. Since then he's had 27 books published. He is the author of *Bullets for a Ballot* and *Coffin for Cash*, both books featuring Cash Laramie and Gideon Miles. His writing guide *Write a Western in 30 Days*, has reviewers recommending it for writers of all genres, not just westerns. His most recent books are *Mission: Prague, Mission: Tehran* and *Mission: Khyber* in 'The Tana Standish psychic spy' series, *The Bread of Tears*, a crime novel featuring a nun who used to be a cop, *Chill of the Shadow*, a modern day vampire thriller set in Malta, and *An Evil Trade*, a crime thriller set in Tenerife.

Also available by NIK MORTON

Write a Western in 30 Days—with plenty of bullet points!
"Morton has a brilliant way of condensing a great deal of information into manageable junks without sacrificing clarity or content. The resulting book works both as master class and as a refresher course."

"This is an excellent look at the writing process. It covers nearly everything and the advice contained here will apply to any genre."

A Fistful of Legends (Editor)
Sudden Vengeance
Spanish Eye
Blood of the Dragon Trees

- The Tana Standish psychic spy series
The Prague Papers (#1)
The Tehran Text (#2)

- The Avenging Cat series
Catalyst (#1)
Catacomb (#2)
Cataclysm (#3)

- Westerns writing as Ross Morton
The Magnificent Mendozas
The $300 Man
Old Guns
Blind Justice at Wedlock
Last Chance Saloon
Death at Bethesda Falls

- Fantasy writing as Morton Faulkner
Wings of the Overlord
To Be King

NIK MORTON Westerns from BEAT to a PULP books:

COFFIN FOR CASH

As a favor to his boss, Cash accompanies a rich woman in her search for her brother. The trail leads to The Bells, a strange hotel run by a brother and sister team, which just happens to be adjacent to the funeral parlor and cemetery ... Meanwhile Miles discovers his charge might be innocent, and lingers in town to ask questions, upsetting some people, and leading to a final reckoning at the outlandish casino complex constructed by a rich, bigoted German baron. Throw in the attractive Berenice, a schizophrenic bank manager, irate miners, Chinese workers, a boisterous slot machine salesman, and a devious lawyer and you have another explosive adventure for the Outlaw Marshal.

BULLETS FOR A BALLOT

In the town of Bear Pines, Mrs. Tolliver has announced she is running for the mayoral office. She's the first woman to run as a candidate which divides the residents and sets the town into a tailspin. U.S. Marshal Cash Laramie is sent in to maintain peace and order and to protect Tolliver and her family from powerful allies of the incumbent, Mayor Nolan. In a bid to force her to quit the race, things turn ugly ... and deadly. Surrounded by killers who will stop at nothing to make sure Mrs. Tolliver is not elected, Cash wires Cheyenne for assistance, but will help arrive in time?

DON'T MISS THE FIRST KNIGHTLY AND COLE ADVENTURES ...

CARNOSAUR WEEKEND by Garnett Elliott

Policing the timelines has always been dangerous, but the brave agents of Continuity Inc. have arguably the most important job in human history. Protecting human history. Newly promoted agent Kyler Knightly teams up with his uncle, Damon Cole, to stop unscrupulous developers from exploiting the Late Cretaceous. A luxury subdivision smack-dab in the middle of dinosaur country threatens not only the present, but super-rich homeowners looking for the ultimate getaway.

APOCALYPSE SOON by Garnett Elliott

Continuity Inc. agent Kyler Knightly and his uncle, Damon Cole, travel back to Old Vegas, circa 2035, to nab a rogue scientist bent on turning pre-apocalypse America into his own personal demolition derby. It's monster trucks versus monster preppers in a nitro burning, high octane adventure reminiscent of Mad Max.

www.beattoapulp.com

www.ingramcontent.com/pod-product-compliance
Lightning Source LLC
Chambersburg PA
CBHW051833170626
46807CB00003B/1152